Her heart was thumping so crazily inside her chest that all the blood seemed to drain from her body, leaving her like a limp rag doll in his arms.

That was until she came to her senses, felt the tenor of the kiss change into something even more dangerous, something even more potentially *explosive*—and became terrifyingly aware that every honed-to-perfection muscle and granite-like inch of his devastating body was pressed as intimately close to hers as a body could be, making them virtually inseparable.

Grappling with the urgent need to set herself free, as well as to stay right where she was and accept the earth-shattering consequences that contact with him wrought throughout her body, Caroline shoved against the implacable hardness of his chest and abruptly disengaged from his tormenting embrace.

'No!'

The terror in her voice sounded unrecognisable to her. Having no choice but to let her go, Jack smiled tauntingly against the back of his hand where he had started to wipe away her taste, as though it was somehow beneath him to bear it. Her eyes stinging with outraged, furio   g defencelessly, she   t seductive allure of   t how powerfully and   c attraction had assert

The day **Maggie Cox** saw the film version of
Wuthering Heights, with a beautiful Merle Oberon and
a very handsome Laurence Olivier, was the day that she
became hooked on romance. From that day onwards
she spent a lot of time dreaming up her own romances,
secretly hoping that one day she might become
published and get paid for doing what she loves most!
Now that her dream is being realised, she wakes up
every morning and counts her blessings. She is married
to a gorgeous man, is the mother of two wonderful sons,
and her two great passions in life—besides her family
and reading/writing—are music and films.

Recent titles by the same author:

THE MEDITERRANEAN MILLIONAIRE'S MISTRESS
THE WEDLOCKED WIFE

THE PREGNANCY SECRET

BY
MAGGIE COX

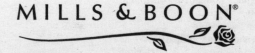

MILLS & BOON®

All the characters in this book have no existence outside the imagination of the author, and have no relation whatsoever to anyone bearing the same name or names. They are not even distantly inspired by any individual known or unknown to the author, and all the incidents are pure invention.

First published in Great Britain 2006
Harlequin Mills & Boon Limited,
Eton House, 18-24 Paradise Road, Richmond, Surrey TW9 1SR

© Maggie Cox 2006

ISBN-13: 978 0 263 84861 8
ISBN-10:   0 263 84861 2

Set in Times Roman 10½ on 13¼ pt
01-1106-43286

Printed and bound in Spain
by Litografia Rosés, S.A., Barcelona

THE PREGNANCY SECRET

To Gary
with all my love

CHAPTER ONE

ALL DAY long the ocean had called to her. At a minute past five-thirty in the afternoon Caroline closed the shop, mounted her bicycle and pedalled with all the urgency of a prisoner making a jailbreak down to the beach. When she got there she left her bicycle in the usual place and all but ran down to the water's edge, breathing in the sharp, salty air with increasing need—as if she had indeed been imprisoned in a dank, dark cell and deprived of clean fresh air for too long.

That was why she knew she could never live far from the sea. On some unexplored, mysterious level it had become part of her. It didn't matter what type of day she'd had, it was the only sure-fire thing that seemed to have the power to rejuvenate her and somehow help put her world to rights.

Caroline didn't know why she'd woken up feeling so intensely restless that morning. There seemed to be no good reason for her sudden strange inability to concentrate or even conduct a simple exchange with any of the customers who came into her little shop for art supplies. Yet she couldn't deny that there was a niggling disquiet deep within her that wouldn't go away—a disquiet that would act like a cattle prod until she relented and gave it the attention it deserved.

There had been plenty of work for her to do in between customer visits too, but because of her state of mind Caroline had barely applied herself to any of it. All she'd done all day was glance longingly at the clock, torn between displaying the 'Closed' sign on the front door and escaping down to her favourite little cove or painting out her agitation onto canvas.

In the end she had acceded to neither of those options.

Now, studying the white-capped waves breaking over the rocks, inching further and further onto the sand like an encroaching colossal army of silver-backed ants, she was taken aback by the intolerable ache that climbed into her throat. If she was honest, she'd been trying to suppress that ache all day, but now—in the one place where she could freely give vent to her feelings—she no longer tried to fight it. It was an old, familiar ache that had its inception in events that had occurred seventeen years ago, and sometimes she wondered at its power to still affect her with such savage intensity.

But Caroline didn't want to start any emotional excavating right now. She would simply allow the feelings to temporarily deluge her, then slowly ebb away again. Just like the tide that so fascinated her. She had escaped to the sandy cove which she had come to secretly regard as her own private oasis hopefully to derive some peace from her unwelcome discontent of spirit, and diving into the past too deeply would surely only visit on her the very *opposite* to that.

All she could do was plant her feet as firmly as she could on the shifting sand, gaze out to sea and *breathe*. This same technique had anchored her so many times in the past, when despair had almost driven her out of her skin, and it would anchor her again today...

Jack hadn't been back to this place for *years...seventeen* years, to be exact. Now he saw that the small coastal town that had haunted his dreams at night had more or less stayed doggedly the same. Summer was long gone, and it was coming on to winter. Thankfully there were no noisy arcades or stands selling sugar candy, as he'd feared—no burger bars polluting the pure sea air with unsavoury aromas, and the population hadn't discernibly increased. *Not to his eyes, anyway.* It still appeared to be the same unassuming and quiet, almost nondescript seaside town that it had always been. The march of time had not rolled over it and left it unrecognisable.

The knowledge made Jack feel so hollow inside that for a moment anyone close enough to study his face would have seen the hard glitter of tears sheen his riveting blue eyes. Perhaps it would have been better if it *had* changed? At least then he wouldn't be so relentlessly attacked by memories that he'd sooner bury for good and forget. Now, the sight of a familiar row of buildings facing the beach, in much the same weathered state that they had been seventeen years ago, and a bend in the road that led to the small cul-de-sac where he had lived with his mother, brought it all back in an unforgiving tide of recollection.

One memory in particular stood out like a beacon in the dark amongst all the rest. *Jack's first ever sighting of Caroline Tremayne.* She'd been walking home from school with her friends, and his youthful attention had been immediately dazzled, entrapped, enchanted by her beautiful smiling face, her long, curling blonde hair, and the most sensational pair of legs that ever graced a pair of school regulation black tights. *He had been under a spell from the moment he'd seen her, and not once since had his heart beat so hard and furious at the sight of a pretty girl…*

Shoving his hands further down into the deep pockets of his Burberry raincoat, Jack walked on, suddenly glad of the soft steady rain that wet his lashes and made his dark hair sleek as a pelt. He told himself she must be long gone from the small town where he had grown up, having moved there with her family the year that she'd turned sixteen. Most likely she had got married to some ambitious young doctor with the blessing of her father, who had been a local GP, and had probably gone to live either in the Home Counties or some gentrified borough in London.

Continuing his speculation on how her life had unfolded without him, Jack wondered if she'd ever done anything about her interest in art, as she'd intended, or whether instead she'd been content to stay home and raise a family while her husband concentrated on *his* career.

The thought automatically slowed Jack's brisk stride right down and with impotent rage he scraped his fingers through his sodden dark hair. He *despised* the fact that the thought of her being with somebody else still had the power to unglue him—to make his heart beat as fast as a rally driver taking a dangerous bend way too fast. Having to make billion-dollar decisions for his companies was a walk in the park compared to the tormenting, blood-stirring and heartrending memories he had of Caroline Tremayne. And the brutal truth of the matter was that she didn't *deserve* him devoting even one second of the time he stupidly spent thinking about her. Not when she had blighted his capacity to trust for ever by what she had done to him seventeen years ago…

Telling himself to snap out of his dark mood and concentrate instead on the main reason he had come back to this place, Jack started to walk on again, his pace determinedly resolute as he headed for the bend in the road that would take him back to the once dilapidated Victorian semi-detached dwelling that he had grown up in…the house that he now *owned* outright and could do with what he damn well pleased…

The driving rain had cut short Caroline's emotionally charged but somehow vital trip down to the sea. Negotiating the roads home on her bicycle, she blinked rapidly into the ensuing downpour, clenching her teeth as wind and rain stung her cheeks and cursing her luck that she should forget to bring her waterproof. Her light cotton jacket was no protection against such an onslaught from the elements.

Startled by a car driving too fast, coming down the street towards her, she jumped off the saddle and steered her bicycle onto the pavement instead. She wasn't far from where she lived and would simply walk the rest of the way. She began to increase her pace—head down, her freezing hands gripping the bicycle handlebars— and didn't see the man walking just as rapidly in the opposite direction towards her until it was too late and they unceremoniously collided.

His hands immediately shot out to steady himself, gripping her upper arms with a hint of steel in his hold as Caroline careened right into him—the front wheel of her bicycle catching him hard against the shin. He swore out loud, not sparing her blushes, and Caroline began to apologise profusely, blinking up at him in alarm and regret.

But as her dark, fair-lashed eyes locked onto the astonishingly vivid blue of the stranger's unrelenting waves of shock hit her like a high-pressure fire-hose—the ferocity of it almost knocking her over. *Oh, my God...*

'Jack?'

Her throat almost locked as she let the name out. She'd forbidden herself the use of it all these years, and now, in one blinding, devastating second, it was out there...just as if it had been waiting to be let loose for the longest time...

'Caroline.' He blinked the rain from his eyes, staring back at her with neither warmth nor pleasure, his hard jaw visibly tightening, as though having been dealt the most unwelcome of surprises.

His frigid, glacial glance cut her to the quick, and Caroline wanted to weep for all eternity at the sheer hostility she saw directed towards her. Instead she grazed her teeth anxiously across her bottom lip, immobilised by shock and distress, wanting to walk quickly away from this cruel encounter fate had dealt her, but somehow unable to make the necessary move to do so.

He abruptly let go of her arms. 'You've hardly changed at all' he ground out, almost as though resenting the observation.

Inside, Jack's senses were spinning and wheeling, his body protesting in silent agony, as though he'd fallen from a great height onto broken glass. What was she doing here? Surely she didn't still live here after all these years? If he had suspected for even one second that of all the people he might possibly bump into from his past Caroline Tremayne would be the first he would *never* have set foot in the place again...never mind returned to buy the house he had grown up in!

He had loved and then *hated* her, with equally voracious passion, and now all he felt for her was ice-cold disdain. But as Jack held remorselessly onto his low opinion he couldn't deny the unsettling evidence of her disarming beauty—a beauty that hadn't faded in the slightest in all the time that had passed...that had in fact blossomed into even more *heartbreak.*

Her skin was still as fine as the most expensive silk, her dark caramel eyes bewitching as an eastern princess, and her mouth...devoid of lipstick and tempting as sin, with that delicately plump lower lip glistening damply with rain... Apparently it still wielded the power to make Jack burn to taste it again.

'What are you doing here?' she asked him now, her hands curving tightly round the handlebars of her bicycle, the knuckles paler than pale.

'That's *my* business.'

'I'm sorry, I—'

'You remember I never *was* one for small talk?' he said, raising an openly scathing dark brow.

Caroline stared. Hot, embarrassed colour surged into her face at his mocking remark.

Jack nodded, one corner of his hard mouth lifting with what might well have been satisfaction at her visibly acute discomfort. 'Well...nothing's changed.'

Digging his hands deep into the pockets of his raincoat, he started to walk on.

'Goodbye, Caroline.'

'Is Dr Brandon finished for the day?'

'His last patient's just left, Miss Tremayne. Why don't you go on in?'

Not giving herself a moment's opportunity to change her mind, Caroline swept past the obliging receptionist to knock briefly at Nicholas's door, and at his auto-matic 'Come in' let herself inside.

The man who had been her father's best friend and closest confidante right up until his death was now hers, and as her agitated gaze fell upon his calm, smiling and familiar face she only just about held onto the last vestiges of composure that had so irrevocably unrav-elled at the sight of Jack Fitzgerald.

'Caroline!'

He walked round the large oak desk that occupied a fair portion of the room space and, pulling her towards him for a hug, kissed her fondly on the cheek as well.

'What a lovely surprise! I was just thinking about you.'

'You haven't any brandy, have you? Purely for me-dicinal purposes, you understand.'

She laughed a little harshly, blinking back the scalding sheen of tears that surged helplessly into her eyes.

Nicholas frowned, his steady, concerned gaze locking immediately onto her clear distress. 'What's happened? You're wet, and shivering too…blasted weather! Come and sit down and talk to me.'

Hurriedly pulling out the chair in front of his desk—the one reserved for his patients—Nicholas saw Caroline settled into it before pulling open one of the capacious drawers and extracting a bottle of best malt.

'No brandy, I'm afraid, darling, but whisky should do the trick just as well.'

Pouring her a generous measure into a small tum-bler—also retrieved from the desk drawer—he handed it to her, the grooves at each side of his mouth deepening as he watched her tip the glass towards her lips and drink.

'This is so unlike you. You have me quite worried,' he confessed, briefly squeezing her shoulder.

Feeling the whisky burn inside her, Caroline winced. After just a couple of seconds the uncomfortable burning sensation became surprisingly pleasurable and warm, providing a welcome if brief respite from the intense anguish she'd suffered since literally bumping into Jack just half an hour ago.

Turning her troubled dark eyes towards Nicholas, she offered him a shaky smile. 'You must think I've completely gone off the rails, or something. I'm sorry to land myself unannounced on you like this.'

'Caroline…we've been friends for a long time now…*good* friends since I lost Meg last year. You know if you're in any sort of trouble I'm always here for you, don't you?'

She knew that he meant it. Nicholas Brandon had been a rock for her since she'd lost her father. She had never seen him as a substitute parent, but her relationship with him and his wife Meg had helped her foster a sense of security that for a long time she'd lacked. When her father had died, Caroline had sorely grieved for the affection she had never had and had always longed for. Her friends had all been in London, and Nicholas and his wife had been unstinting with comfort and support when she'd decided to move back to her old home. But Caroline had never spoken about Jack Fitzgerald to the

kindly couple before. Had never told them how, at
sixteen years of age, she had fallen deeply and passionately in love with the man and would have willingly
followed him to the ends of the earth if only he'd given
her the chance…

But Jack had had a burning desire to rise above his
family's troubled and debt-ridden daily existence and
make a fortune for himself. And after events that had
changed the course of both of their lives for ever he had
followed that desire to America. *But what had brought
him back here?*

At their very last meeting, when he'd all but torn out
Caroline's heart with the vitriolic tirade he'd lambasted
her with, telling her that he would never set foot in
England again, she'd been convinced that he truly meant
every word he had uttered. He *hated* her for what she
had done, and was never, *ever* going to forgive her. And
if his reaction at their unexpected meeting today was
any indication, he clearly still saw no reason to rescind
his promise… Her throat tightened with agonising hurt
at the memory.

'I appreciate—I appreciate that, Nicholas, but I'm
not in any trouble…really. I've just had a bit of shock,
that's all.'

Nursing her glass between her hands, Caroline stared
down at her lap.

'What kind of a shock?'

'A ghost from the past…only he's not really a ghost.
He's flesh and blood and bone.' *And once upon a time*

I loved him so much my days were consumed with thoughts of nothing but him...

'Are we talking about an old boyfriend, perhaps?'

Lowering himself onto the desk next to her, Nicholas put his hand thoughtfully up to his jaw, a subtle draught of the classic cedarwood-scented aftershave he wore briefly stirring the air.

'I can see that you really are shaken up, darling, so it must have been someone who meant something important to you once upon a time.'

'He wasn't a boyfriend.' Caroline shrugged, the dampness from her thin cotton jacket making her shiver. But she also silently acknowledged that shame factored somewhere in there too. 'At least...not in public.'

By necessity she'd had to keep her relationship with Jack as secret as possible, because her father had issued dire warnings to her when he'd inadvertently found out she'd been seeing him. He wasn't from their world, he'd told her and when it came to prospective boyfriends he expected someone much, much better for his only daughter—not the son of a junkie and a drunk.

Three months later, when she'd just turned seventeen and found herself pregnant with Jack's baby, Caroline had had to confess to her father the truth that she'd been seeing him in secret.

Terrified, because Jack had already told her of his plans to make some 'big money' in the City, which would naturally necessitate him moving to London, and that nothing was going to stop him, Caroline had seen all her options dwindling before her eyes. *She hadn't wanted to hold her boyfriend back in any way. She knew what he'd endured and she'd only wanted the best for his future.* So, buckling under brutal pressure from her enraged father, Caroline had brokenly agreed to have an abortion.

When she had told Jack what she had done his love for her had immediately turned to *hatred. He'd never forgive her,* he'd promised and then he had sworn that he would never see her again.

Until today, he had kept that vow.

'Are we talking about Jack Fitzgerald?'

Caroline glanced up in shock, the colour leaching from her face at Nicholas's painfully astute question. 'You *know* about him?'

'Your father was my closest friend, my dear. Of course I knew about your infatuation for that boy.'

That 'boy' was now a man of thirty-seven—three years older than Caroline.

A startlingly vivid picture of his disdainful handsome face less than an hour ago, now etched with distinct grooves in his forehead, and with bitter lines bracketing a mouth that once upon a time had been devastatingly sensual and charming instead of frighteningly forbidding, flashed up in her mind. A jolt of deep, bruising sorrow almost made her moan out loud.

'Then you…you know what happened?'

'That you were expecting his child and had to have an abortion? Yes, my dear…I know about that.'

Thankfully, there was no criticism evident in Nicholas's

voice, and he left Caroline to her own preoccupied thoughts for several seconds, before following up his quiet matter-of-fact statement with a deeply thoughtful sigh.

'Your father thought it was the best thing to do at the time—and he was right. You were only just seventeen, Caroline, with your whole future ahead of you. He wanted you to go on to university and study, find a career you would love. He knew that a boy like Jack Fitzgerald would never have stood by you. You would have been a single mother, raising a child on your own, while your friends were doing the very things your father wanted for you. He really loved you, you know.'

'Did he?' Tears were like a thick net curtain, blurring her vision, as Caroline stared up at the man beside her. 'If he had really loved me, Nicholas, would he have put me through an abortion at seventeen years of age? Wouldn't he have stood by me and helped me when I found out I was pregnant, instead of condemning me and helping the man I loved to despise me for ever?'

'He tried to make amends by leaving you the house, and enough money to set up in business,' Nicholas asserted, quietly yet firmly—his steadfast loyalty to Caroline's father was unwavering.

Rising disconsolately to her feet, Caroline delivered her glass to the small leather coaster on the desk. Tossing back her mane of curling blonde hair, she sniffed, regarding the man beside her with distinct hurt in her eyes.

'He hardly ever told me that he loved me,' she told

him. 'I could count the number of times on one hand! Do you really think that leaving me a house and money could come anywhere *close* to making amends for such a grim lack of affection, as well as helping me to lose my baby and driving Jack away?'

When Nicholas said nothing in reply, Caroline inclined her head briefly in sorrow.

'I should go home now. I shouldn't have come here and burdened you with all of this.'

'Your troubles are not a burden to me, Caroline, and they never *could* be. I would do anything I could to alleviate your pain...you know that.' Taking her small cold hand in his own, Nicholas squeezed it tight with genuine fondness. 'But, whatever the reason Jack Fitzgerald has returned here, I really think it best if you don't get involved with him again.'

Extracting her hand as though it had glanced against burning blue flame, Caroline immediately backed away and walked stiffly to the door.

'I know you mean well, Nicholas, but you can save your advice. If I lay unconscious on the ground Jack Fitzgerald would step over me...never mind get involved! He despises me for what I did. When I saw him again today I could see it in his eyes.'

CHAPTER TWO

AFTER thrashing out some of the finer details with the contractor he'd hired to oversee the renovation work, Jack left the house that had once been his childhood home, jumped into his car, and drove along the coast for several miles without really paying much attention to where he was going.

Emotionally he was under seige. Seeing Caroline again after seventeen long years had made the blood stampede through his veins like escaping wild horses.

But after almost an hour of aimless driving, and feeling no less overwhelmed, Jack pulled in to the side of the road, switched off the voice of the DJ on the radio that had been droning monotonously in the background and, staring out through the windscreen, vocalised his mounting frustration out loud.

She had no right to look so gut-wrenchingly beautiful…to taunt him with the fact that clearly life had been kind to her since they had broken up. Jack couldn't bear to imagine that her undimmed radiance was the result of a happy marriage with a man who *adored* her—who would have *died* for her as once upon a time Jack willingly would have.

He had fallen so hard for the blonde dark-eyed beauty that her unexpected act of treachery had all but *killed* him. Since then relationships had come and gone, and although his life had by no means been devoid of sexual passion there hadn't been the love that Jack had instantly felt in his heart for Caroline. And now, since his divorce from Anna last year, he was alone again.

Rubbing his chest beneath his shirt, he sucked in a harsh breath to steady himself.

Despising the pulse of fear that jolted through him, an aggravating thing that seemed to happen a lot these days since his heart attack, he continued to stare out through the windscreen.

The surrounding countryside, with its timeless and arresting beauty, should have helped instil some calm inside him—but no such luck. Jack was a million miles away from calm today, and expecting it to suddenly arise was a fruitless undertaking...no matter *how* long he sat there. *All he felt was empty.*

He'd come back here to set right a wrong. To prove to himself and the town that despite his poor beginnings, and the mostly negative perceptions people there had had about him, he had achieved success beyond their wildest dreams. He was a multi-millionaire entrepreneur, with several thriving companies to his name and a much-admired reputation for proving that there was still a place for integrity and not just flair and daring in business. That admiration had massively highlighted Jack's profile in the international business community, and had won him the cover of the *New Yorker* just one year ago.

It was the kind of dreamed-for reputation that should have long ago rubbed out the taint of his boyhood shame—of having an alcoholic father who had abandoned his family and a mother who had heavily relied on prescription drugs to sedate her from the hurt she'd known was waiting if she should try and face her days without them. But Jack had to silently acknowledge that seeing Caroline again—the sight of her cruelly reminding him that she had not thought him good enough to be the father of her baby, and had preferred to have an abortion rather than raise their child together—had frankly robbed him of the sense of triumph at returning home that he'd been hoping for.

But he had laboured too hard and too long for success to let this unexpected, glitch completely quash his satisfaction at buying the house that had once belonged to his parents but had been repossessed for non-payment of the mortgage. That unhappy and shameful fact had forced Jack and his mother to be housed in run-down council flat accommodation on the outskirts of town, and had no doubt helped contribute to her growing despair and eventual demise. Now that the place was his again, Jack's plans were to have it converted into a stunning showpiece of a home that would elevate it into one of the most desirable properties in the area—*in any area*—and would obliterate every bruising, shameful memory that might still be lurking there from his past.

His mother might no longer be alive to witness his achievement—but he wasn't going to let that stop him from seeing through the burning desire that had gripped him with a vengeance while he was recovering from surgery in hospital six months ago, after suffering his heart attack. But how was he going to deal with the startling discovery that the girl who had broken his heart when he was just twenty was still living in the area? It was definitely a complication he hadn't foreseen.

'Goddamn!'

Colouring the confined space with his invective, Jack impatiently switched on the ignition and roared out of the lay-by, as if by putting his foot down hard on the gas he could outrun the threatening cloud of his own troubled past…

'My idea was to make a collage of butterflies…'

'I'm sorry, what did you say?'

Guiltily, Caroline brushed back her hair with her hand and deliberately focused her attention on the pale young teenager in front of her, a swift upsurge of concern galvanising her attention. A shy, unconfident girl, Sadie Martin had latched onto Caroline at the school where she taught arts and crafts once a week and now regularly visited her shop—often with no other aim in mind than to chat.

'I said I wanted to make a collage of butterflies.

They're so beautiful, don't you think? I got some books from the library to study them.'

A soft, self-conscious tinge of pink seeping into her naturally milk-pale complexion, Sadie sighed wistfully—as though her dream of creating something beautiful out of butterfly imagery was somehow just out of reach.

Caroline empathised. She knew what it was to have a dream that was out of reach. Once she had dreamt that she and Jack would be together for ever, but it had all ended in a dreadful nightmare. Now that he was back she found herself dreaming about him again…only this time there was no prospect of a happy resolution, or even the *remotest* possibility of one. He had clearly hardened his heart so emphatically where she was concerned that he found it difficult to even look at her, let alone converse.

All morning Caroline had speculated feverishly about why he had come home. Would he be staying long? *Would he ignore her every time their paths accidentally crossed?* It was only a small town—it was inevitable that they would. She didn't think she could bear to see that despising glance he had swept her with for a second time.

'Well…' Diverting her own unhappy thoughts, she levelled a tender smile at Sadie instead. 'Books are a good place to start if you want to study butterflies. But if you want to start work on a collage why don't you look through some magazines for pictures you can cut out? I have a pile of them at home I could bring to class on Friday for you, if you like?'

Sadie's pale lips edged upwards. 'Would you? Oh, that would be great! My mum doesn't read magazines, and I can't afford to buy them myself.'

'I tell you what…I'll help you get started, if you like. I've got loads of material scraps out at the back of the shop that you can have. You'll be able to create something really amazing.'

'That's very kind of you, Miss Treymayne.'

'I told you…call me Caroline.'

'All right. I'll see you on Friday, then…at school?'

'I'll look forward to it…and, Sadie?'

'Yes, Miss?'

Smiling at the automatic barrier of formality that the girl could not so easily relinquish, Caroline reached out to tenderly smooth away a stray auburn hair from her earnest young face.

'Any time you need to talk…I'm here for you, okay?'

She knew it wasn't the 'done thing' to encourage pupil/teacher relationships outside of school. But, remembering her own sense of abandonment and isolation living with her father, Caroline believed that everyone deserved a helping hand now and then, as well as emotional support—and there was something about Sadie Martin that indisputably tugged at her heartstrings.

'Thanks, Miss.'

The bell over the door briefly jangled, and Caroline stood alone in the ensuing silence and reflected how hard it was to teach someone how to have self-confidence at the tender age of sixteen. God knew it was enough of a challenge sometimes even at thirty-four!

Jack had been walking with no particular aim in mind other than to reacquaint himself with his home town. When he left the main street and turned into a series of charming connecting lanes—the chocolate-box imagery of typically pretty English country villages springing immediately to mind—his pulse accelerated sharply as he came upon a small shop with a bright blue, painted frontage and a swinging sign that declared 'Caroline's Paintbox'. He knew before he even glanced in the window and saw her serving a customer, amid picture frames and paintings decorating the walls, that the purveyor of the business was none other than the woman who had been haunting his dreams all these years…

He hadn't intended to go inside, but before he knew it Jack's hand was gripping the brass handle on the front door and he was stepping into a colourful treasure-trove of paints and paintings, pencils and stencils, racks of handmade occasion cards, artists sketchbooks and much more besides.

The customer Caroline had been serving—a middle-aged woman, immaculately dressed in a smart pearl-grey trouser suit—smiled almost girlishly at him from beneath her heavily mascaraed lashes as she passed him. A waft of Chanel No 5 impinged strongly on his senses. But the woman's smile glanced off Jack like water sliding down glass, hardly registering with him at all. All his attention—all his focus—was intently on Caroline.

'Just a minute and I'll be with you.'

She was bundling up some unwanted paper and depositing it in the bin with her back to him as she spoke, clearly unaware of who her next customer was. She straightened again, a ready welcoming smile on her it had to be said radiant face. The smile vanished almost instantly when she saw that it was Jack.

'Was there something you forgot to be rude to me about?' she asked stiffly, her arms folded defensively across her chest in her chocolate-brown wool sweater.

'I was passing and saw the sign with your name on it. I wondered if this might be your place.'

Deliberately avoiding looking directly into her wary brown eyes, Jack instead took inventory of his surroundings, minutely interested in every detail—every corner and every crevice overflowing with artistic implements of one kind or another—simply because this venture belonged to Caroline. *Was this what she had done with her love of art?* Somehow he told himself it didn't sit right. The Caroline Tremayne he remembered hadn't been a facilitator of other people's artwork—she'd created her *own.*

Back then, she'd been bursting with excitement and ideas about what she was going to do when she finished art college. Her aim had been to eventually have a fantastic studio overlooking one of the London parks 'to inspire her' she'd said. Where she would create the most wonderful paintings that she would exhibit in galleries and that the great and the good would admire and hopefully buy.

'Eat your heart out, Leonardo!' she'd used to say with great delight and not a little self-mockery.

Jack had truly believed she'd be a roaring success. Her ravishing beauty and the utter passion she'd exuded for life had swept him off his feet like a sensual cyclone…how could it not have? His mother—during some of her more lucid bouts with reality—had used to tell him that Caroline would break his heart. *Well, she'd been right on the money with that one.*

'Take your time, why don't you?' Her voice was tinged with sarcasm. 'But you'll have to excuse me. I've got work to do.'

When she would have turned away from him again, Jack's next words kept Caroline rooted to the spot.

'Any of the stuff on the walls yours?' he asked, nodding his head towards the three rows of paintings behind him. Her chin came up and her dark eyes glittered, as if she was offended by the question, and Jack knew that if he had been an artist himself he would have been spoiled for choice of which angle to paint her from, because she looked so damn good from whatever perspective you gazed. A sizzle of molten heat carved a direct path south in his anatomy and made him feel momentarily dizzy.

'No. These days I paint purely for my own satisfaction, but not for public viewing.'

'Why not?'

Characteristically blunt, Jack levelled his clear

blue gaze on Caroline's startled face with no remorse whatsoever.

'I can be freer if I only have myself to please. I make art because I take pleasure in it…not because I want other people's opinions about it.'

'You used to want to make it your full-time career'

'Well, now I have this shop—and I teach too. That's quite enough to be going on with.'

She was prickly and defensive, yet she still painted—even if it was just for her own satisfaction—and apparently did lots of other things as well. Clearly what had happened had not quelled her drive in any way…neither had the fact that their romance had so abruptly come to an end. The thought did not sit easy in Jack's already disturbed gut.

'What do you teach?' he asked reluctantly.

'Arts and crafts. Are there any more questions? I have to get on.'

Jack frowned at the distinct coolness in her voice. 'I didn't expect to find you still living here,' he commented, changing tack.

'I moved to London for a while, but then my father died and left me the house. When I came home to sort things out I decided to stay here. I love the sea…it's always had a pull for me.'

Caroline hadn't meant to tell him so much. It had just sort of come out, due to nerves. Because here she was, having not seen this man in what felt like a lifetime, and there he stood, frighteningly mature and handsome in his casually expensive clothes, the body inside them clearly having had the benefit of not just good genes but good nutrition and exercise too, judging by the strongly athletic build of him. His appearance was a far cry from the lean and hungry energetic youth she had fallen in love with, who'd had a burning desire to break the bonds of his less than advantageous background and make both his fortune and a name for himself. But, with his disturbing blue eyes searing her like living flame, it seemed to Caroline that his dangerous attraction was even more potent than ever. Why else would she be standing in front of him privately shivering hard with longing?

'So…is there a husband somewhere on the scene?' he asked, looking as though he couldn't care *less* if there was.

She could ask him the same question. Are you married Jack? And if you are…why have you come back here to haunt me? Once the question entered her mind Caroline found it hard to let it go. She had a dangerous fascination in knowing the answer.

'No… How about you? Did you ever marry?'

Her voice shook with nerves as she gave in to her own helpless curiosity.

'I'm divorced. So…neither of us is a success in the marriage stakes…surprise, surprise.'

A knot of unbearable misery twisted inside Caroline's stomach.

'Why are you doing this, Jack? You already told me that you hate making small talk. You don't need to come in here and rake over old coals when the past is better left alone…don't you think?'

His face grew briefly dark, and the bitter tension that rolled towards her hit Caroline like an icy wave. She knew immediately what he was thinking. He'd made a bad mistake coming into her shop and making contact again, and now he was sorely regretting it. There was not one thing he'd missed about her...not *one*. Watching him walk to the door, she saw Jack shrug, and before pulling it open he considered her with a supercilious and definitely mocking smile.

'Your father died, then? Forgive me if I can't bring myself to offer my condolences.'

Without another word, he left her alone.

The large Victorian house that her father had left to her in his will, which for the past five years had been Caroline's permanent home, failed to inspire her usual pleasure as she entered the airy hallway with its chequered floor and polished chiffonier. All of a sudden it didn't feel like home, because her normal ability to experience delight in things had been severely suppressed by Jack's cruel parting remark when he'd left her shop.

Not that she could entirely blame him for not being sorry to hear of her father's death.

Charles Tremayne had disliked Jack on sight, calling him a 'sly little upstart' who only wanted to elevate himself by association with Caroline because she was a doctor's daughter and came from a different class. For different read *better.*

Her father's unapologetic snobbery and prejudice

had made Caroline feel intensely ashamed. They might have been more comfortably off than Jack and his mother, but that hadn't given them the right to feel superior in any way. Right from the start Caroline had quickly seen that Jack was smart and industrious, as well as devastatingly good-looking. And he might have appeared as a bit of a cocky, brash youth to outsiders, but to her he had displayed a tenderness that had sometimes made her weep for joy. Having grown up with a father whose affection towards his only child had been sparing, Caroline had found Jack's loving like a salve to her starved-for-love soul. *Once experienced...nothing else would do.*

Sighing with deep unhappiness, Caroline dragged herself into the kitchen. With her mind constantly drifting back to the past, like a wary onlooker positioned on the edge of a dormant volcano, she prepared a baked potato and a small salad for her dinner. Eating it in the large, formal dining room a little while later, she stared at the dark emerald drapes at the imposing Victorian windows and asked herself what she was doing, still rattling around in this big old house on her own after five years? Why had she rebuffed every bit of interested male attention that had come her way, as if she didn't deserve to find happiness with a man who loved her? *She knew the answer to that one.*

After he'd found out about the termination, Jack's fury at her had known no bounds. His passionate, enraged words, eloquently expressing what he thought of her, had slashed deep wounds in her heart that would probably *never* heal. He had made her feel like a murderer…as if she had made the decision to terminate her pregnancy on a mere casual whim. He had had no idea of the guilt, shame, or total devastation Caroline had felt when, at her father's bullying instigation, she had gone through with the deed. He had had no notion of the terrible scene her father had caused when he'd found out about the pregnancy, *or* the dreadful names he'd called her for sleeping with Jack. Events like that left an indelible imprint on a person that was hard to relinquish. Caroline had found it almost impossible to forgive herself for what had happened, and because of her guilt had subconsciously put up barriers where other men were concerned.

'Oh, Jack' she said out loud as her fork clattered back down to her plate, her meal still left largely untouched. 'Why did you have to come back? I've made a life for myself since you went away… Maybe I'm not the successful artist that once upon a time I thought I could be, but I've been happy in my own way with the shop and my teaching. Why did you have to come back and spoil that? Why couldn't you just let the memory of you die in me for good?'

CHAPTER THREE

HAVING had negotiations with the architect who was overseeing the renovation and redesign of the house, Jack left the hotel where he was staying the next morning and went for a long walk along the seafront. Dressed in black sweats with a matching fleece, he tried to quash the need to run that arose inside him—to pound the pavements as he was used to doing every day back in Manhattan, where he lived and worked—because since his heart attack the doctors had advised him to 'kick back a little' and not push so hard with the exercise regime he'd devised for himself.

Resenting their advice like hell, Jack nevertheless had to satisfy himself with a brisk walk rather than a run, and as the surprisingly cold autumnal air bit into his hollowed-out cheekbones he found himself recalling his parting words to Caroline yesterday. *It had been a stupid and childish response to have a cruel dig at her about her father's death,* he decided. No matter how vehement his dislike for Charles Tremayne and the appalling way he'd treated Jack back then—as if he was nothing less than *pond-scum*—Caroline had no doubt loved her father, and missed him not being around.

It surprised him that he should seriously be considering giving her an apology. If he had an ounce of sense he'd leave things be and not try to see her again. *But Jack never had been able to do the sensible thing around Caroline.* How else had she wound up pregnant with his baby at just seventeen? The pavement seemed to loom dizzyingly closer for a second as he remembered how much he had loved her, how *crazy* for her he had been from the moment he'd seen her. She should have been off-limits to him right from the start—and *would* have been if her dark eyes hadn't gazed at him with equally desperate longing at their very first meeting.

Increasing his stride without thinking—his heart maintaining a steady, reassuring rhythm as he did so—Jack made himself concentrate on the exercise. He knew he was getting fitter by the day. The heart attack—though disturbing and a cause for concern—had thankfully not been life-threatening. It had, though, been a *warning* that he couldn't afford to treat his body's innate need for rest and relaxation with the near *contempt* with which he'd treated it previously.

'You're not some battery-powered *machine,* Jack Fitzgerald…a battery runs out and you replace it with another one. The body doesn't work like that. You can't work flat out seven days a week, getting by with the minimum of sleep indefinitely, without it exacting some kind of price on your health.'

His doctor had been right, of course. But after Jack's marriage had started to come apart at the seams—and Anna had naturally sought solace elsewhere—Jack had preferred to spend his time at work and take his chances with the toll on his health. To his mind it had been infinitely easier than going home to a luxurious penthouse apartment and having the empty rooms that were mockingly bereft of his wife's presence chillingly remind him that this was one arena in which he patently *didn't* excel…

Slowing to a stop, he ran a hand across the thin film of sweat clinging to his brow and returned to the knowingly dangerous idea of making contact with Caroline to apologise for his rudeness of yesterday. She might not have wanted to have his baby all those years ago, and he could never forgive her for what she'd done, but there was no need to stoop to the condescending level of her father and treat her with anything less than civility. After all…she was *nothing* to him now. What could it hurt to merely drop by her shop and say sorry for his ill-mannered passing quip?

She didn't have a head for heights at the best of times. Now, on a ladder reaching up to the topmost shelf in the back room where she kept her stock, searching for that box of material odds and ends that she'd promised to Sadie, Caroline sighed with relief when she found it, only too eager to get back down the ladder and onto *terra firma* again.

But as she drew the large box towards her chest to balance it her foot missed the next rung it had been groping for and she felt herself literally crash to the floor. Releasing a shocked yelp, she landed unceremoniously on her backside at the foot of the ladder, the box of material scraps spilling out everywhere. Cursing her bad luck, Caroline groaned out loud in pain and frustration—because she could already feel the bruises forming on her most tender spot.

Hearing the jangle of the bell above the shop door at that exact moment, she rolled her eyes heavenwards. 'Great timing, Caroline,' she muttered. Pushing away the colourful kaleidoscope of debris that covered her, she attempted to rise to her feet. *Everything hurt.* The place on her body that *didn't* hadn't been invented.

Hobbling to the door, and at the same time trying to smooth back her dishevelled hair as she went out into the shop, she was totally unprepared for the sight of Jack, leaning against the counter examining a box of crayons as though they were the most fascinating thing on earth. He straightened when he saw her, and Caroline saw the grooves on his handsome forehead crease in a frown that was unexpectedly concerned.

'What have you done to yourself?'

It wasn't fair that he of all people should walk in the door and catch her at her most vulnerable. *Someone up there in the cosmos was having a big joke at her expense.* If that wasn't bad enough, Caroline knew she must look dreadful too. Apart from nearly doing herself some serious damage falling off the ladder, she was wearing a pair of jeans that were just on the uncomfortable side of tight, and a smock-type Indian print blouse she was convinced she looked fat in but that she'd worn anyway because it was roomy.

She'd been in the middle of cleaning the stockroom when she'd remembered the box of material scraps she'd promised Sadie for her butterfly collage. Knowing it was dusty work, she'd thought it best to change into clothing that she didn't care about. Now, with her hair shaken loose from the bold pink scrunchie that had kept it on top of her head, and practically every bone in her body screaming in silent protest from her undignified tumble, all Caroline wanted to do was to be left alone to entertain her humiliation in private. What she expressly *didn't* want was to be under the despising scrutiny of a man who clearly thought she wasn't fit to be in the same room as him—never mind be spoken to.

'I'm all right. I accidentally fell off a ladder, that's all.'

With her hand shaking, Caroline tried in vain to push her hair back from her face, but the stubborn silky strands spilled heedlessly back across her cheeks again.

'You *fell* off a ladder?'

Before she could do anything to stop him, Jack had walked commandingly over to her and clamped his hand down firmly on her shoulder. His blue eyes were as intense as she'd ever seen them as they blazed down at her.

'Are you hurt? You look like you're in shock… What the hell were you doing up a ladder on your own?'

The question was so surprising that Caroline's lips couldn't help twitching into a perverse grin. 'What do you mean? Since when does a person need an escort to go up a ladder? That's taking it *too* far, if you ask me!'

'I don't think this is any time for joking,' he said seriously, wiping the smile off her face with his chilly reprimand. 'You'd better come and sit down. Do you have anything for shock?'

A double vodka might do the trick if she had any, Caroline reflected in sudden panic. Still holding onto her shoulder—the heat from his hand was making her feel almost delirious—Jack guided her to a nearby straight-backed chair with a floral seat-pad and gently but commandingly pushed her down into it. Just when she didn't think she could cope with his painful concern for her welfare one second longer, without it making her dissolve into sorrowful, angry tears, he stood in front of her with his arms folded, regarding her with all the forceful presence of a commander in the SAS towards a member of his team who had badly let him down.

The thought would almost have made Caroline smile if it hadn't been for the sober reminder to herself that he would *never* in a million years want her on his team.

Glancing tentatively up at the harsh jaw—that was distinctly unshaven this morning and made him look almost dangerously unpredictable—and seeing his expression of searing inscrutability made Caroline literally squirm in her seat.

'I asked you if you had anything for shock?' he repeated.

She shook her head, knowing that it wasn't just because he was standing and she was sitting that he had a distinct psychological advantage.

'I don't believe in taking medicine unless I really have to. I've got some Rescue Remedy in my bag, but that's about all.'

'Rescue remedy?'

'It's a flower remedy…very good when you've been upset.' Caroline's stomach lurched as Jack surveyed her with an almost tangible sceptical air.

'You'd rather take some dubious alternative remedy over an orthodox one and your father was a doctor?'

'I *do* have a mind of my own, you know.'

As soon as the words were out of her mouth, Caroline painfully recalled caving in to the pressure from her dictatorial father to have the termination she'd had…*despite* her vehement protest that she didn't want to, that she *loved* her baby and she loved her baby's father. It hadn't helped her having a mind of her own then—not when her father had crushed her insistence with all the rough and pitiless force of a sledgehammer.

Painfully, she swallowed down the inevitable, almost unbearable twist of loss and grief inside her and attempted to rise up from the chair. *She had to make Jack leave, and leave now!* What was he doing here anyway? Surely he had better things to do than visit a woman who aroused nothing but *contempt* in him?

It bothered Jack greatly that he'd witnessed such disturbing vulnerability in her soft dark eyes. Let her show him indifference, or even tell him to go to hell, but dear God don't let her look as though she was suffering the torments of the damned.

It frankly astounded him that the idea of Caroline being in pain still had the power to bring out the protector in him…even after what she'd done. He told himself to take a swift reality check and get the hell out of her shop and her life for good. Just because the sight of her still had the power to stir explicit male fantasies in him—her snug, faded jeans emphasised that her figure had lost none of its charms and had inevitably become even more womanly and alluring than ever—it didn't mean that he should stay around any longer than was sensible. *He'd already been burned by her.* He didn't intend to be burned again.

'You need a little more reliable help than a flower remedy, in my opinion. Don't you have the common sense to keep a first aid kit here?' Jack asked impatiently, irked because he felt more affected by her presence than he wanted to be.

'I do, but it's only got bandages and plasters in it. Please don't give it another thought. I'm fine, really.'

'You could have broken your damned neck!'

The tension in him suddenly too extreme to stay contained, Jack threw Caroline a fierce look. He heard her shocked intake of breath at his vehement outburst.

'Well, how inconvenient for you that I didn't!' she

came back at him, a distinct catch in her voice despite her seeming bravado.

'I don't deny that I wanted you to suffer after what you did, but I'm hardly likely to want you to kill yourself.'

Deeply affected by the grating quality in his voice, Caroline felt her anxious gaze stare up at him, mesmerised.

'One day you were telling me that you were pregnant with my baby, and the next that you'd had the pregnancy terminated. Talk about a kick in the head, Caroline!'

Her whole body protesting in pain, Caroline dug her nails into her palms, as if deserving of even more. She wanted to tell Jack about her father…how he had *forced* her into having the abortion…but what would telling him such a thing achieve? Jack's reaction would probably be to despise her father even more—and maybe even her too, for being too weak to resist his coercion. She could hardly bear any more of his contempt.

She sucked in a deep breath. 'You were planning on going away… I knew how desperately you wanted to change your life for the better, to make some money and free yourself, and I—I was only seventeen, Jack.' She shook her head in an agony of searing emotion, feelings surfacing that for seventeen years she'd had to lock away deep inside her, in a cast-iron trunk with chains and a padlock, in order to stay sane. 'I—I was afraid.'

'You should have talked to me…not just gone ahead and done what you did.'

Jack couldn't even bring himself to say the words *You*

killed our baby…the miracle that they had created out of their passion and love. He just about managed to rein in the fury and pain that was surging through his blood like a fiery contagion. She might have been afraid, and just seventeen years old, but still he couldn't help but feel cruelly betrayed that she hadn't come to him and asked his help to work things out.

It didn't matter that he'd had that feverish desire to escape the small, going-nowhere town where he'd grown up… He'd been in deep shock when she'd told him she was pregnant. He would have definitely delayed his desire for flight if Caroline had only asked him to—if she had not made such an irreversible decision on her own. In any case, he had planned for her to move in with him just as soon as he'd got himself established and she'd finished her education… They'd *talked* about it enough times, for God's sake! She'd known he wasn't playing a game with her—she'd known that his feelings for her were all-consuming and completely genuine…

'Can we stop this? Can we stop this right now? I really don't want to talk about the past any more. I have to get back to work… And although it might look hunky-dory from the outside, you shouldn't be so quick to assume that my life has been nothing but a breeze since you left.'

Determinedly Caroline got to her feet, despite feeling dizzy and sick and close to wanting to die right then. There wasn't one emotion Jack could display that she didn't feel acutely. *She hated it that she'd hurt him so badly.* If she could somehow turn back time she would—just to undo that one heartrending deed. But she couldn't. And she'd clearly received the message that Jack was still no more *near* to forgiving her for what she'd done than he had been all those years ago, when they had both been so young.

The agony of that realisation seemed even more raw than it ever had been…like a blister that would never heal. All Caroline could do was live with it as best as she could—just as she'd been living with it all this time, until his shocking reappearance.

'Why did you come back here to see me, Jack? There's nothing for you here.'

She was absolutely right, of course. There was nothing he wanted from Caroline Tremayne ever again.

Trying to clear his head, Jack forced himself to remember why he'd sought her out.

'That comment I made yesterday about your father…I'm sorry. It was uncalled-for.'

'You came to apologise about that?' She looked dumbfounded.

'How did he die?'

'In his sleep…he had a brain aneurysm.'

'Did he suffer?'

He saw her wrestle with the answer, suspicious of his interest, probably wondering if he was only trying to be malicious. *Damn!* He had no business being concerned one iota at how she was perceiving him! All he needed to do was close the conversation and get the hell out of there as quickly as he was able—not prolong the undoubted agony of their meeting one moment longer.

Brushing back her tumbled hair, Caroline briefly surrendered her defences and met Jack's gaze head-on. 'Thankfully, it must have been very quick and very sudden. Nicholas—a friend of ours who's also a GP—told me he wouldn't have suffered at all.'

'Good.'

Turning on his heel, Jack started to walk away. He told himself the only reason that he stopped halfway to the door was that she'd suffered a fall and he had to be sure she was properly okay. He utterly refused to entertain the renegade idea that the sight of her was stirring up that old dangerous attraction he'd harboured for her so long ago, and knew that if he had the remotest instinct for self-preservation he'd better keep a good distance between him and her for the remainder of his stay—for *however* long that might be.

'You ought to get yourself checked over by the doctor after having that fall off the ladder. Sometimes there can be internal injuries you can't see.'

Oh, God, did she know about those! Unable to handle his rough-voiced concern for her well-being another moment, Caroline smoothed her hands down her jeans, fiddled with her hair and cleared her throat determinedly to give her the courage to stay strong.

'Really, I'm fine. I don't need to see a doctor. I'm disgustingly resilient. Rubber bones, don't you know? I bounce right back when I get hurt.'

A curious expression she couldn't read crept into Jack's inscrutable blue eyes at her flippant words.

'How fortunate for you,' he remarked, his lean jaw tightening with a visible jerk. In less than half a minute he'd exited the shop, leaving the mocking tinkle of the little bell above the door sounding more like a cacophony of gunshot behind him than gentle, wistful chimes…

'No bones broken, thank goodness, but you should have come to see me straight away after it happened. You've got some nasty bruising and stiffness, that's all, and that will heal in a few days.'

Walking round his desk, Nicholas strode over to Caroline, where she stood after her examination, pulling on her jacket.

'Let me take you out to dinner…you look as though you could do with a little TLC.' He touched his palm to her cheek, his hazel eyes crinkling at the corners with both concern and humour.

With her own doctor away, Caroline had reluctantly asked Nicholas to check her over. Jack's words about seeing a doctor had been ringing in her ears when she'd woken this morning—barely able to get around with the bruising on her hip and thigh that she'd suffered from her fall. But, truth to tell, most of her misery had been more to do with the fact that Jack still blamed her for having the termination than any physical bumps and bruises she'd suffered. She'd woken in the night wishing with all her might that she had stood up to her domineering father more and refused the abortion he'd insisted on.

Now, her thoughts returned irrevocably to Jack. His appearance had created all kinds of mayhem inside her. There was no question that whatever he'd done and achieved it had been a resounding success. His clothes were of the very best quality—Caroline had seen that straight away—and he had the accomplished, confident air of a man who had diligently shaped his own destiny. *But there was also an edgy desolation in his eyes...as if all he'd achieved wasn't nearly enough to quell the deep unhappiness he harboured within himself.*

'Dinner?' she repeated, her mind reluctantly breaking away from thoughts of Jack.

'I'll pick you up at around eight. Try not to look so unhappy, darling...a few bruises won't do you any lasting harm.'

Forcing a reluctant smile to her frozen lips, Caroline nodded in agreement. 'I know. I'm just annoyed at myself for being so stupidly clumsy, that's all. I'd love to go out to dinner tonight. Thanks, Nicholas.'

'You're not still fretting about Jack Fitzgerald being back on the scene?'

Unable to keep the disapproval from his voice, Nicholas returned to his desk.

Feeling her stomach plummet to her shoes at the mention of the man who had been dominating her mind for the past three days, since his return, Caroline's reply was vehemently dismissive.

'Of course not! It's all in the past, and I got over him a long time ago. I was only upset when I saw you because it was such a shock to see him again like that. Like I said…I'm over it now.'

But as Caroline said her goodbyes to Nicholas and went to the door, she thought, with a little sigh of despair, *You're such a hopeless liar, Caroline Tremayne.*

CHAPTER FOUR

IT WAS one of those seaside hotels steeped in the elegance of a bygone Victorian era, yet brought unobtrusively up to date with all the trappings and conveniences of contemporary life. It had a fabulous Michelin-star-winning restaurant much beloved by both local visitors and those who travelled from further afield. Caroline liked to have afternoon tea there sometimes—not so much for the delicious cucumber sandwiches and mouthwatering selection of cakes, but more for the ambience. She would sit in the lovely drawing room, with its proud antiques and unapologeticiliy faded English grandeur, and dream the time away until it was time to leave.

She rarely had dinner there, so—in deference to dining out with Nicholas—Caroline had raided her wardrobe for something a little more dressy. Her red and white chiffon dress, with its sequin-inlaid scooped neckline, lent elegance and grace to her curves, and in defiance of the anxiety she'd suffered over the past few days she'd painted her lips with vibrant scarlet lipstick. Nicholas had told her she looked lovely, and the genuinely kind compliment had given Caroline a much needed boost. She definitely needed her friend's more positive response after her dealings with Jack yesterday afternoon.

'Some wine, darling?' Perusing the leather-bound list at their table, Nicholas lowered it for a moment and smiled.

'You choose.'

Caroline knew it was the reply he was expecting. Nicholas Brandon epitomised 'old-school' chivalry—his undoubted good manners underscored with an unapologetic dose of masculine chauvinism. It was the background and era he came from, and Caroline knew she shouldn't be offended in any way. On the other hand, when her father had employed similar attitudes—often to demonstrate his power over her—it had completely rubbed her up the wrong way.

She glanced unhappily down at her menu, the writing seeming to swim and blur in front of her eyes at the unwanted memory. It was when she lifted her head up again, glancing round the room in a bid to bring her spiralling mood back into more positive check, that she spied Jack, sitting alone at one of the tables on the far side of the room from them. A tall sash window with oyster-coloured drapes provided an elegant backdrop to his clearly preoccupied appearance as he glanced straight ahead of him absently nursing his wine glass—apparently regarding nothing in particular.

Sucking in her breath deeply with shock, Caroline promptly sent her menu flying off the table, taking her own empty wine glass with it before she could prevent it. The glass tumbled to the thickly carpeted floor but thankfully did not shatter into pieces—as her composure was busy doing. Automatically she dropped to her haunches to retrieve it, along with the menu, her hand trembling as her fingers circled round the stem, all the blood roaring inside her ears at the realisation that Jack was dining there too.

On the other side of the room Jack's attention was diverted by a beautiful blonde in an eye-catching red and white chiffon dress, crouching down by her table to retrieve a fallen glass. When she glanced up, and Jack's gaze fell helplessly into her dark-eyed caught-in-the-headlights stare, his insides tensed in astonished surprise.

Caroline!

It was as though the concentration of all his thoughts for the past hour—which had been about her—had miraculously summoned her physical appearance, and Jack was genuinely stunned. As she sat down again, deliberately averting her gaze, he saw to his chagrin, he glanced across the table at her companion. The man was clearly much older than Caroline. At a guess Jack would have said late fifties at least. *Who was he? Surely not her current boyfriend?*

Jealousy seared his blood like the excruciating slash of a whip across his bare flesh. The man was old enough to be her father, and Jack didn't like the proprietorial air he had about him as he leant over and reassuringly squeezed her hand after she'd picked up the glass. Acting purely on instinct, Jack was on his feet and striding across the richly furnished dining room towards them before he even realised that that was what he intended.

'Hello, Caroline.'

To Jack, it was as though her companion didn't even exist. When she glanced up, startled, into his face, her cheeks pinkening in obvious embarrassment at his direct address, he was transported back to their first proper meeting—when he'd asked her what her name was and then told her that she was the most beautiful girl he'd ever seen. She'd blushed in the same unknowingly sexy way then, and he had been gripped by a fever of wild longing so profound that he had known meeting her would make an impact upon his life for ever. *He hadn't been wrong about that.*

'Jack.'

Pulling her glance away, she delivered what seemed to Jack to be an apologetic frown at the man on the other side of the table, and it made his blood boil. It reminded him of the condescending, superior way her father had once regarded him…as if he was the dirt beneath his feet.

'Aren't you going to introduce me to your friend?'

For now, he refused to assume that the man was involved with Caroline in any meaningful way. It simply did not bear thinking about.

'Of course.' She tried for a smile, but the gesture barely touched her scarlet-painted lips for a scant second.

Jack could see that he had put her immediately on edge. *Good. He wanted to put her on the defensive. He wanted her to suffer the way he had suffered when her father had humiliated him by telling him he wasn't good enough to go out with his daughter.*

'This is Dr Nicholas Brandon. He was a good friend of my father's.'

Jack smiled easily at the other man's clear and instantaneous dislike, feeling somehow gratified that Caroline had introduced him as her father's friend but *not* specifically *hers*...

'Nicholas...this is Jack Fitzgerald.'

'Indeed.'

Even though Nicholas rose to his feet, to briefly and reluctantly shake Jack's hand, Caroline could tell straight away that his view of Jack had been indelibly corrupted by her father's opinion from way back. It made her furious. Nicholas had no right to treat Jack with anything but courtesy and respect. He didn't even know the man, for goodness' sake!

'Pleased to make your acquaintance,' Jack responded, smooth as silk—the slight drawl in his otherwise English accent denoting he'd spent a long time on the other side of the Atlantic. But, no sooner had he mouthed the insincere platitude, he diverted his attention straight back to Caroline. 'You're looking pretty as a peach,' he remarked, shocking her rigid with the unexpected compliment. 'What's the occasion?'

'There is no special occasion, as such,' Nicholas interceded with irritation, his hazel-eyed glance seeming to issue Caroline with a silent reprimand for even deigning to introduce him to her one-time boyfriend. 'We are merely two friends having dinner together. Now, if you don't mind excusing us…'

Caroline could hardly believe that Nicholas was dismissing Jack so rudely. Her sense of justice and fair play would not allow it—no matter how contemptibly Jack might treat her for past misdemeanours.

'Have you had your meal yet?' she asked him, silently terrified at what she was about to propose. 'You're welcome to join us if you'd like.'

To say that Jack was surprised by the invitation that issued from her very distracting lips was putting it mildly. Uncaring that the other man might register his definitely over-familiar and possessive glance as he let it travel from her face down to her shoulders, then lower, he felt bold, naked lust rip into him like a sword. The scooped neckline of her alluring red dress couldn't help but call attention to the firm ripe breasts that were contained within it, and the ruby-red pendant she wore nestled tantalisingly in the shadowy valley between them.

No wonder Dr Nicholas Brandon wanted her all to himself! Caroline might fool herself that her relationship with this man was platonic, but Jack could see from a mile away that the man lusted after the sexy brown-eyed blonde as much as *he* did. The fact that Jack didn't even pause to question the wisdom of desiring Caroline's body again after all these years, and after the damage she'd done, didn't even impinge upon his consciousness right then. All he knew was that he had to have the chance to get her back into his bed again…*even if it was a one-time only deal.*

'I'll have to pass,' he replied in answer to her question, and briefly but deliberately smiled knowingly at the visible relief in her companion's eyes. 'I'm going to have my coffee, then go up to my room to do some work. Another time, perhaps? No doubt we'll be bumping into each other again.'

'You're staying here at the hotel?' Caroline asked in surprise.

'I am. Oh, by the way…how are the bruises from yesterday?'

Knowing that he was acting as if he'd been intimately acquainted with the sight of them, Jack played up to Nicholas Brandon's evident annoyance with relish.

'You *know* that Caroline had a fall?' the other man demanded, his expression accusing.

'I was there just after it happened. She always *did* have a tendency to be a little accident-prone…didn't you, Caroline?'

His voice grew deliberately husky on that last statement, and his blue eyes burned into Caroline's panicked dark gaze with the kind of hot sparks that started forest fires. *She turned boneless and hot in an instant.* Jack had always had the disturbing ability to look at her and make her feel as though she were practically having sex with him at just a glance. *But why should he regard her like that, when he'd already made his dislike of her crystal-clear?*

In spite of her confusion, Caroline could barely tear her gaze away from him as he leant towards her and provocatively brushed the side of her cheek with his lips. The stubble on his jaw lightly scratched the delicate tenderness of her own soft skin, and the smell of his cologne acted like a flame-lit arrow fired straight into her womb. Inside her dress, Caroline's breasts grew exquisitely tender and achy.

'Did I?' she answered nervously, embarrassed to recall a tendency to be clumsy in front of both men. But, that aside, she couldn't believe that Jack had kissed her. It had been seventeen interminably long years since she had known his touch, and now that the drought had ended she couldn't help but feverishly crave *more*. She felt an intense surge of joy rush into her blood, despite knowing that her craving was probably doomed to remain unsatisfied.

'Well...I'd better be going.' Sending her another maddeningly provoking glance—that made Caroline's breath catch and seemed to suggest that he had a lot more on his mind than coffee and work—Jack turned and left her alone with her clearly disgruntled dinner companion.

Had he meant it when he'd commented so casually that they would be bound to bump into each other again? Or had he simply said it to annoy Nicholas? Caroline suspected that Jack had taken an immediate and intense dislike to the man who was a family friend and wondered why. Maybe it was the association with her father that irked him? Maybe he'd intuited that he must have been the subject of some discussion between them at some point in the past, and of course strongly resented it. Certainly Nicholas had made no effort to hide either his negative judgement *or* his disdain for Jack.

When Jack had walked away from them, Nicholas wasted no time in warning her for a second time about seeing him again.

'If you know what's good for you, Caroline, you'll steer clear of that man,' he said disapprovingly across the table. 'I'm rarely wrong about people, and I confess I don't particularly trust him. To my mind he can bring you nothing but trouble.'

She resisted the urge to hotly disagree, because underneath the profound agony of need that was burning anew for Jack in her blood Caroline silently conceded that her friend was probably *right*. What if Jack was up to something? What if seeing her again had prompted the idea of some kind of *revenge* in his heart for what she'd done?

Wondering how she was going to eat when she'd completely lost her appetite, Caroline merely toyed with her delicious meal when it came, until it was time to go…

The following day, having finished teaching her Friday arts and crafts class, Caroline hurried to catch up with a distracted-looking Sadie Martin as she headed out of the school gates, feeling a stab of concern that needed answering. In fact, the girl had been dreamy-looking all through the afternoon's lesson, and had not given her work her usually eager attention.

Thoughts of Jack suddenly banished, Caroline released her brightest smile as she drew level with the schoolgirl. 'Hey, there! You're in a big hurry…going somewhere nice?'

Slowing down her stride, Sadie guiltily dipped her head and blushed furiously.

Caroline's undoubted curiosity as to what might be the matter was piqued even more. 'Is everything all right, Sadie?'

The girl waited until the sea of girls behind them surged through the gates ahead of them, then continued a little way up the road with Caroline before gradually slowing to a stop.

'Everything's fine, Miss…really.'

It was the *really* that spoke volumes to Caroline. Her dark eyes narrowed in concern. 'Do you want to talk? We can go to the park, if you like? I'm not in any hurry.'

'Thanks, Miss…I'd like that.'

There was a flash of gratitude in the girl's surprised glance, and Caroline intuited she'd done the right thing in catching up with her.

In the park, after finding a suitable bench situated beneath a large sheltering oak that was liberally shedding its golden and brown leaves on the grass beneath it, Caroline surveyed the younger girl with another undeniable throb of concern as she sat down beside her.

'I've met a boy…a boy I—I like very much.'

Her concern expanded into a disturbing lightning bolt, and Caroline stared in astonished surprise. It was the *last* thing she would have expected Sadie to say, and for a long moment she just sat there, bereft of words.

'Miss?'

'So…' Caroline cleared her throat, then took a deep breath to calm the wild fluttering in her stomach. *Sadie was sixteen*…the same age Caroline had been when she'd lost her heart to Jack. 'When did all this happen and how did you meet?'

Again, Sadie's pale complexion was suffused with visible heat. 'I've been seeing him for about a month now. His name is Ben and he goes to the local art college. A friend of mine has an older sister who goes there, and she got us tickets for a dance they were having. That's when we met.'

'He's obviously older than you if he's at college?'

'Only by three years, Miss…that's not much of an age difference, is it?'

'No.' Quickly gathering her scattered wits, Caroline combed her fingers through her mane of blonde hair. 'That's not much of an age difference at all. So now I know why you've seemed particularly distracted lately. Is everything going all right? Have your parents met him?'

'Yes, they have. I wouldn't see him behind their backs, Miss! Besides…I'm not one for going out much usually, and lately…well…I've been going out quite a lot, so they'd immediately know that something was going on if I didn't tell them. My dad likes him very much, as it happens…and my mum's slowly coming round to the idea that I've got a boyfriend…I *think.*' Sadie shrugged self-consciously. 'She's a bit of a worrier, my mum. I think she's afraid that I might get into trouble.'

'What kind of trouble?' Even as the words left her mouth Caroline knew that Sadie meant becoming pregnant. For a moment anxiety made it hard to breathe. *Oh, God, don't let history repeat itself,* she thought in anguish. Sadie *deserved* her bright future, untarnished by the pain of a romance that had gone wrong or a man who'd rejected her before she had really even grown into a woman…

She took another deep, steadying breath. At least Sadie had parents who loved her…who would in all likelihood stand by her should things go wrong. It was a very *different* scenario from her own cautionary story.

'You know…I meant getting pregnant, Miss.' Her pale hands tightening around her dark blue school bag, Sadie grimaced a little. 'But even though I'm only young, I'm much more sensible than my parents give me credit for. Ben and I are just really getting to know each other still. We haven't slept together, and when and if we do I'll go to the doctor and get protection. I won't jeopardise either of our futures.'

'That sounds…extremely sensible, Sadie.'

Swallowing hard, Caroline forced a smile to her lips. *If only she and Jack had been nearly so sensible…* But unassailable passion had made them its willing slave, and they'd been like pieces of driftwood afloat on a stormy ocean of insatiable lust. The word 'sensible' hadn't even been in their vocabulary. Her stomach flipped over at the bittersweet memory.

'But even when you're trying to be sensible, sometimes things can get a little out of hand. You know that the Head of Sociology at school—Glynis Hopkins—does relationship counselling for teenagers? Why don't you go and have a word about things with her? She's very kind, and anything you tell her will be in the strictest confidence, I promise.'

Sadie's face lit up with touching beauty. 'Thanks, Miss…it's been great to have you to talk to. I knew you'd understand.'

If only I didn't understand half so well, Caroline reflected painfully as she reached out to squeeze Sadie's hand. 'As your teacher and your friend I only want you to be happy,' she replied softly.

Later that evening, although on edge, and once more consumed by thoughts of Jack after Sadie's revelation that she was seeing a boy, Caroline did not have the heart to visit the little cove in search of some calm. Instead she opted to go for a drive—anything to try and distract herself for a while.

Usually the ocean would call to her whenever she was remotely upset, but not *tonight*. She was simply feeling too anxious about the parallels she'd drawn with Sadie to even summon up the energy to walk on a deserted beach. Instead she drove by it, barely even glancing over at the waves that were splashing onto the shoreline.

The evening was drawing in, and the air had the sting of frost in it when she finally returned home and parked the car on the drive. Retrieving her bag from the passenger seat beside her, she locked up, then proceeded to walk wearily up to her front door.

'Do you usually stay behind this late at school?'

Her heart in her mouth at the sound of that voice, Caroline felt her knees react as though they might fold like paper beneath her—just like a marionette when the puppet-master stopped working the strings. Spinning round in shock, she found Jack just a scant foot behind her, his face unsmiling, his blue eyes seeming to drill into her like lasers.

'Jack! What are you—? How did you know I was teaching today?'

Feeling a hot shiver go right through her, Caroline helplessly focused on his mouth—on the little diagonal scar just above his top lip that he'd acquired when he was seventeen, after a fight with another boy who'd had a flick-knife. The way Jack had told it, the boy with the knife had come off far worse than he had, and had never bothered him again after that night. Looking at him now, Caroline could *easily* believe it. To her, he had always been like *electricity*...utterly necessary, but at the same time *dangerous* and unpredictable too... No doubt that teenage boy had completely underestimated what Jack was capable of.

'I knocked next door and asked your neighbour.' He smiled, but the gesture lacked warmth. Instead it was the lethal, purposeful smile of a man who knew he had the upper hand where she was concerned…would *always* have the upper hand as long as she couldn't resist him. 'She was most obliging too.'

Nicolette was an attractive forty-something divorcee who regularly combed the lonely hearts ads in the local paper with steely-eyed determination, in search of 'husband number three'. Caroline didn't doubt she had been only too happy to tell Jack practically *anything* he wanted to know. But—as much as she was over-whelmed by his presence—she wasn't up to raking over old coals tonight, if that was what he had in mind. *Like the boy who had attacked Jack with the knife, she knew she would come off the loser.*

Clutching her bag to her chest, Caroline frowned, secretly longing to get out of the biting wind and into the warmth of her centrally heated house. 'What is it you want? It's—it's cold out here.'

'Then why don't you invite me in?'

Stepping towards her, Jack shrugged beneath the ex-pensive leather of his dark brown jacket, the material making a soft creaking sound as he raised his arm and pushed back his hair.

Confusion, then resignation crept into her expressive eyes. Jack couldn't deny his moment of triumph. He'd had a very brief moment of doubt, when he'd thought she might refuse him, but the tension between them

was palpable and he knew immediately how to manip-
ulate it in his favour. *She was as jumpy as a newborn
kitten around him,* he realised, *and he had no compunc-
tion…none…in taking the utmost advantage of the fact.*

'All right, then…just for a minute.'

The house was warm and inviting, and Caroline's
perfume—a mixture of jasmine and roses, if Jack wasn't
mistaken—lingered enticingly in the air. It was the kind
of home that Jack had dreamed of living in growing up.
There was a real sense of permanence and beauty about
it, which no doubt Caroline's artistic soul had liberally
contributed to over the years.

Following her into the spacious hallway, he watched
her hang up her jacket and bag on the coatstand and free
her long curling hair from the back of her knitted cardigan,
where it had become trapped. The perfectly blonde curls
unravelled down her back with a jaunty bounce, and Jack
had to slip his hand urgently into his jacket pocket to
prevent himself from acting on the almost irrepressible
urge to grab a handful of those luscious curls and twine
them possessively round his fingers…

Turning to face him, she clearly had no inkling of the
impulse that had gripped him so hard. 'Would you like
a cup of tea or something?'

He had a mind to tease her… to ask her what she
meant by 'or something' and insinuate a very *different*
agenda to the one on offer. But when Jack studied that
beautiful and, it had to be said, *guileless* face of hers,
he was suddenly filled with the memory of how devot-

edly and ardently he'd loved her, and how she had taken that pure, passionate love he'd offered and destroyed it in one shocking, irretrievable act...

'Jack?'

He shouldn't have come. But he'd been as unable to resist seeking Caroline out again as a drug addict was unable to turn down a free fix. He was playing a dangerous game that could only end in unqualified disaster, but he asked himself what he had got to lose when he'd already lost everything that truly meant anything in his life a long time ago.

'Tea will do fine,' he said, combing his fingers through his dark hair. But he said it without a smile, and he knew that she knew too that the past had suddenly bitterly intruded into his thoughts.

Crestfallen, she lowered her liquid dark gaze and turned determinedly away. 'I hope you don't mind drinking it in the kitchen,' she threw over her shoulder, her voice falsely bright as she hurried ahead of him down the long, echoing hall...

CHAPTER FIVE

'YOU'VE obviously got a good reason for being here, Jack, so why don't you tell me what it is?'

Cupping her hands around her hot mug of tea at the kitchen table, Caroline decided there was nothing for it but to face head-on whatever was on his mind. She'd spent seventeen years racked with an inordinate amount of guilt about what she'd done…guilt and *fear*…so much so that she had been unable to form a lasting relationship with anyone. Every time she'd tried…every time she'd met someone she'd started to feel herself attracted to and who had been attracted to her…it hadn't been long before that dreadful burden of guilt and terror had submerged any growing feelings of pleasure or hope in the relationship continuing, and eventually— *inevitably*—it had come to an end.

Hadn't she carried that debilitating burden for long enough? Her heart *longed* to be able to love again, to give itself wholeheartedly to the right man without fearing that she might fall pregnant and be forced to terminate again. But, looking into Jack's stare—Caroline was convinced it was contemptuous—it was obvious he didn't think that she'd suffered *nearly* enough.

'You live here alone?' he asked, ignoring the question.

'Yes.'

'I always wondered what this place looked like on the inside,' he commented, glancing around him, his gaze alighting on the beautiful Irish dresser with its eye-catching display of highly collectible blue and white china. 'Your father would never let me over the threshold.'

Feeling shame at the memory, Caroline dipped her head.

'So…you're not in a relationship?'

Her head shot up.

'No.'

She could have said more, but she didn't. Whatever she said, Jack would no doubt draw his own conclusion as to the reason for her still single status anyway, and she didn't need to hear his self-righteous judgements against her.

'So…you and the disapproving doctor aren't an item?' His lip curled slightly as he put his emphasis on the word 'doctor', and Caroline knew he was only looking for an opportunity to 'put her in her place' and keep her there.

Suddenly resentment welled up in her heart, for all the pain he had caused but clearly took no responsibility for, and she could barely speak over the abominable tightness that locked her throat.

'That's totally irrelevant. What interest can it possibly be to you who I'm seeing or not seeing? Let's have this out for once and for all, shall we? You must have looked me up again for a reason and if that reason, is merely to drive home your point that you can't ever forgive me for what happened between us, then save your breath! I already *got* that point—loud and clear. We were both so young when it happened, and we've both moved on a long way since then. You clearly got everything you wanted in life, so why come back here simply to dig up old unhappy memories?'

Leaving her mug on the table, her tea untouched, Caroline pushed to her feet and, hugging her arms across her chest in her dark green sweater, walked unseeingly over to the darkened kitchen window that only reflected back her own unhappy solitary reflection.

She tensed when she heard Jack rise from the table, sensing immediately that he had moved up behind her.

'How do *you* know that I got everything I wanted, huh?'

His voice was hoarse with accusation and Caroline hardly dared breathe. Instead, his rage wrapped itself around her and held her prisoner in an icy vice, so that it was impossible to move out of its powerful sphere.

'All I meant was that you look like you've made a success of your life, Jack… I didn't mean that I—'

'You think because I've got money now, and I'm clearly not the poor boy from the wrong side of town any more, that I'm a *success*?'

Turning towards him, everything in her taut with

trepidation, Caroline was utterly dismayed by the desolate and savagely bleak expression she saw written across his remarkably striking features.

'I—I don't know who you are any more, Jack. I don't know enough about you to assume anything.'

The intoxicating scent of leather from his jacket—an expensive, almost *earthy* smell—mingled with the palpable heat from his body and made a devastating ambush on Caroline's already acutely charged senses. The clock on the kitchen wall ticked with hypnotic precision, lulling her into a kind of frozen suspended animation, and outside somewhere a car door slammed.

When Jack's hands locked fiercely onto her upper arms she dizzily registered the unmitigating *bite* of them with a soft, surprised groan. Then his mouth descended upon hers in a hot, punishing kiss that seemed to be governed by equal parts rage and desire, and Caroline was shockingly reminded that pain and pleasure could be as intimately and destroyingly intertwined as love and hate.

Her heart was thumping so crazily inside her chest that all the blood seemed to drain from her body, leaving her like a limp rag doll in his arms. That was until she came to her senses, felt the tenor of the kiss change into something even more dangerous, something even more potentially explosive, and became terrifyingly aware that every honed-to-perfection muscle and granite-like inch of his devastating body was pressed as intimately close to hers as a body could be, making them virtually inseparable.

Grappling with the urgent need to set herself free, as well as to stay right where she was and accept the earth-shattering consequences that contact with him wrought throughout her body, Caroline shoved against the implacable hardness of his chest and abruptly disengaged from his tormenting embrace.

'No!'

The terror in her voice was unrecognisable to her.

Having no choice but to let her go, Jack smiled tauntingly against the back of his hand. He had started to wipe away her taste, as though it was somehow beneath him to bear it. Her eyes stinging with outraged, furious tears, and her mouth quivering defencelessly as she fought the frighteningly potent seductive allure of him, Caroline was shocked at how powerfully and treacherously the old magnetic attraction had asserted itself between them.

'What the hell do you think you're doing?' she demanded, moving nervously across the room to the door. 'Get out of my house and don't come back! Do you hear me? I want you to go! I want you to go right now and never come back!'

'Still think you're too good for me...don't you, baby?'

The smirk on his lips and the derision in his eyes made Caroline feel quite wretched. But beneath the drowning sensation of despair that washed over her she couldn't believe that he could even *utter* such a calumny with the smallest *grain* of conviction. She had never, *ever* felt that Jack wasn't good enough for her, and she had certainly never treated him like that either. He was quite unfairly getting her mixed up with her father—his fury towards Charles Tremayne blinding him to the truth of her own feelings towards him.

'I've *never* thought I was too good for you! You're twisting things around so that you can heap more blame on me…so that you can make me the brunt of all your old bad feeling towards my dad!' Catching the corner of the door, Caroline pushed it deliberately wide. 'I only invited you in because of plain good manners, but I should have listened to my better instincts and left you standing there! I've had a long day, and now I just want to be on my own and have some peace. Please go, Jack. Just go.'

It was hard to get his feet to move. In those melting, feverish seconds when once again Jack had tasted the irresistible soft satin of the most lustfully sweet pair of lips he had ever kissed all his passion, all his urgent, relentless, *destroying* need for the woman in his arms, had been furiously and frighteningly rekindled. So much so that Jack really didn't know what to do next. To incite some urgently needed self-preservation he ruthlessly reminded himself of what she had so callously destroyed, and as that old hatred towards her helpfully resurfaced, and made another painful score across his heart, he was finally able to move.

'I'm going, Caroline, don't worry.'

Unable to resist stopping in front of her before going out through the door, Jack deliberately took his time examining the wild rose colour that had flared so arrestingly in her cheeks. 'Living alone must be quite a challenge for you. I'd say that you've definitely been without a man too long, sweetheart. I'd certainly put my last dollar on it that that superior doctor friend of yours can't effect the same shamelessly undone expression you're wearing right now with *his* kisses. Am I right?'

When she didn't reply, but glanced away from him instead with a resentful, hurt look in her eyes, Jack laughed softly.

'Don't fret…I'm certain we'll be seeing each other around again quite soon…of that I've no doubt.'

'Why? I should have thought that you'd want to go out of your way to avoid me.'

'What? And deprive you of the beautiful memory of me and our happy times together for ever?'

'You don't have to be so cruel'

'Yes, sweetheart…I do.' Smiling arrogantly, Jack scathingly angled his jaw. 'It helps remind me of your own cruelty towards me.'

As he turned to go, Caroline couldn't resist asking one final question. 'You still didn't tell me why you came back here. I think you could at least have the decency to tell me that much.'

His mocking expression unchanging, Jack shrugged. 'I bought my parents' old house—the one that got repossessed…remember?'

Caroline experienced a heartfelt jolt. 'I remember.' *He'd been enraged about that. She remembered the savage look on his face when he'd told her about it the same night it happened...unhappily recollected that there had been tears in his dazzling blue eyes as he'd told her and how it had shocked her to witness them.* It was then that he'd asserted his intention of leaving this 'Godforsaken place' to make his name and fortune. When he came back, his mother would never be afraid to hold her head up in this 'ignorant, small-minded town' again.

'What are you going to do with it? You're not going to move back there, are you?' Her voice almost dropped to a crushed whisper at the very idea, and she thought wildly that she'd have to move away, or even go abroad herself...*anything* but live in the same small town as Jack Fitzgerald again!

As if sensing her panic, Jack studied her with a deliberate taunt in his fierce blue gaze. 'You're just going to have to wait and see, Caroline...just like everybody else in this town.'

It was when he got back to his hotel suite, his body as restless as someone high on amphetamines from their charged encounter, unable to do anything but pace the floor for several minutes until he'd calmed himself down, that Jack reluctantly recalled the fear and panic he had witnessed on Caroline's beautiful face.

He didn't want to feel the slightest grain of compassion for her obvious distress. He didn't want to remember that she'd trembled like a leaf in his arms when he'd kissed her so savagely—probably scaring her half out of her wits as well as making him almost crazy with desire. But she'd looked so *good*…more than he'd been able to bear…and smelled so divine. She was a fully matured woman now, not a young, innocent schoolgirl, and she was even *lovelier* than ever.

Briefly touching his fingers beneath the bridge of his nose, Jack sucked in a deep ragged breath at the taunting waft of her perfume that clung to his skin. *Dear God! Why did this have to happen to him after all these years, when he'd spent a lifetime trying to forget her?* Why now, when he'd established himself as a man of means, when he could go anywhere, do anything, be with practically any woman he wanted? Why was it that the *only* woman he craved beyond any good reason was Caroline Tremayne? *It was like having an addiction to dynamite. And he didn't doubt that pursuing her in any way would cause his whole life to blow up in his face.*

Dropping down onto the bed and shrugging off his leather jacket, Jack impatiently undid the first three buttons on his black shirt, as if their being closed was choking him, and sat for long minutes just staring off into space, his hand against his chest, beyond furious that he should have to consider the effect of the stress he was suffering on his heart.

Why was it that she hadn't married? Impatiently considering the possible reasons, Jack could have crawled out of his own skin at not knowing the answer. Why was it that she wasn't even living with someone, didn't have a man in her life on a regular basis? Of course she might well have been married and it just hadn't worked out. Whatever. The mere idea that she was single now was enough to conjure up all kinds of impossible dangerous fantasies in his head.

It would have been so much easier for both of them if they'd been involved with someone else, he realised. Jack had a strict code of conduct about fidelity. Even when Anna had been playing around he hadn't retaliated by taking a lover outside of their marriage himself, and he wouldn't have persuaded Caroline to cheat on her husband if she had had one…*no matter how badly he yearned to have her in his bed again…* His father had destroyed his mother with his heartless philandering. His cheating and drinking and lying had driven her to resort to 'medication' to numb her pain. Even as a young boy, Jack had realised that.

'For God's sake! The past is dead and buried…just leave it alone, why can't you?'

Pushing to his feet, he walked across the room and, moving the velvet drape at the window aside, stared out at the quiet empty street below—the silence only broken by the sound of the ocean in the distance. Why *had* he been so compelled to return to this place? There was no salvation for him here…no one except the seller of the house he had bought for too high a price because he wanted it so badly to be glad that he'd returned to the town he was born in.

No…his coming home was *nothing* like he'd once envisaged it would be. The sooner he finished overseeing the renovations on the house the sooner he could leave, return to the life and work that had brought him an undoubted measure of success in the world…an undoubted measure of the *respect* he'd so badly craved as a young man. He should think about that and stop driving himself mad with thoughts of what he *couldn't* have and definitely *shouldn't* want if he knew what was good for him. *And he was damn sure that when he did leave Caroline Tremayne would mourn his going about as much as she'd grieve over some unknown stranger leaving town…*

Like a naughty child who'd been warned about staying away from a place that might potentially bring her harm, Caroline walked surreptitiously down the little cul-de-sac where Jack and his mother had lived all those years ago, glancing guiltily from side to side as if Jack might appear at any second and demand to know what she was doing there. *Truth to tell, she didn't really know what she was doing there herself.* But Jack's telling her that he was having his old home renovated had feverishly sparked Caroline's curiosity, and instead of driving to open up the shop—as she should have been doing—here she was, creeping about like some kind of private detective hoping to get an illicit compromising picture of somebody's wife or husband cheating on their spouse.

Automatically she touched her chilled fingers to her mouth and imagined she could still feel the lingering aftermath from his blisteringly hot kiss of yesterday. *The fevered recollection of that kiss in every detail had dominated Caroline's dreams last night.* Even though she knew all Jack had wanted to do was punish her in some way for what had happened in the past, it hadn't relegated her near-erotic dream to a nightmare, as it should have done. *No—her body had thrashed around in bed, tormented by the memory of his touch as though it would never know peace or rest again.*

Work had begun on the old Victorian semi-detached dwelling with a vengeance, she saw. Besides the huge digger outside, and the crew of workmen going in and out of the front door with wheelbarrows full of bricks and mortar, or busily occupied up scaffolding, a well-dressed man in a beige raincoat and with a bright yellow hard-hat on his head consulted drawings with another man dressed in jeans and sweatshirt with a well-known sports logo on it.

It looked like a huge and pretty serious undertaking, and Caroline could only stand there in wonderment that Jack had made his passionate promise come true... made his fortune and been able to come home and buy the old place where he and his mother had lived their sometimes hand-to-mouth existence.

It hurt her deeply to remember his despair over their lack of money, but even then Caroline had known that Jack would turn his family's fortunes around. He'd always had a Herculean determination to rise above any adversity and turn a disaster into a triumph. It was just too bad and too tragic that his mother had not lived to enjoy the fruits of her son's labour…

But why? Why had he wanted to buy the house and do it up? As far as Caroline knew, he didn't have any family left around there to keep in touch with, and most of his memories of their little town were hardly the kind he would look back on with fondness—so what had driven him to commit to such a strange undertaking?

Telling herself that her curiosity was bound to be left unsatisfied, because relations between them were hardly conducive to exchanging secrets, Caroline turned to walk back the way she'd come. Right now she should just be getting on with her life and enjoying the results of her own personal success. Jack might imagine she'd failed somehow by not making art her full-time career, and he might see her working in the shop and teaching as a poor substitute—but Caroline knew better. She had the best of both worlds. She could still enjoy her painting without earning her living by it, and working in the shop and teaching arts and crafts at the school helped her enthuse and assist others in making their own art.

There was nothing in that arena she should feel remotely ashamed or regretful about. She should certainly not allow her hostile ex-boyfriend to make her feel bad about the way her life had turned out.

Jack was just walking round from what was now a flattened and decimated garden, in preparation for the spectacular transformation that he and his designer had in mind for it, when he stopped, his stomach jolting at the sight of Caroline, walking away down the street on the opposite side of the house. *What the…?* Before he could check his own rash decision, he removed the hard hat the foreman of the site had given him, threw it down amongst some rubble, and ran to catch up with the rain-coat-clad figure down the street.

'Were you looking for me?' he asked huskily, planting himself in front of her so that she was forced to stop.

Digging her hands into her coat pockets, Caroline felt her astonished glance trapped as thoroughly as a rabbit in a snare. She was wearing her hair loose today, and it flowed over her shoulders in healthy and shiny golden curls that, coupled with her shapely figure were already attracting the inevitable wolf-whistles from some of the men on the site.

Glancing round at the direction they came from with a frown, Jack soon had them silenced with an icy admonishment from a reproving blue glare.

'No… I mean, I was—I was just…'

It was no use. *How could she act nonchalant when last night's combustible kiss was clearly in their minds as their heated glances locked?*

She had been *drawn* here as inevitably as moths drew near bright light.

Struggling to maintain her rapidly diminishing composure, Caroline tried to move around him, but Jack touched her coat-sleeve to waylay her.

'I suppose you came to take a look at the house? I'm having some major work done, as you can see.'

Caroline found it near impossible to tear her too-starving gaze from Jack's compelling and mesmerising visage, but she gave the house a cursory once-over anyway—thoroughly embarrassed and ashamed at being caught out showing an interest in his project. An interest that might lead him to believe she still felt something for him after all these years.

The thought electrified her. She should know well enough by now to give him a wide berth—not deliberately put herself in the vicinity of wherever he happened to be! *Hadn't they hurt each other enough without coming back for more?*

'It always was a beautiful old building,' she commented, her face flushing hotly when he continued to examine her with the kind of searing intensity reserved for objects of impossible fascination.

'Beautiful, but dilapidated. There never *was* any money to maintain it back then.'

'Well, I'm sure you'll more than restore it to its former glory.' About to smile, Caroline nervously withdrew the gesture and told herself it was time to go. 'I'm on my way to work and I'm already late,' she explained lifting her shoulders in an apologetic shrug.

Jack helplessly focused in on her lips. She had a mouth that teased and provoked even when she didn't mean it to. A throb of languorous heat radiated straight to his groin. Apart from idle curiosity he had no idea what had prompted her to come and look at the house this morning—*especially* after their passionate clash yesterday—but her appearance told him that she was finding it as difficult to remain immune from him as he was to her.

Amid Jack's undeniable flare of satisfaction at the idea, he knew deep down that their dangerous attraction for one another could only lead to the kind of trouble he should be hell-bent on avoiding…

CHAPTER SIX

'DO YOU take a lunch-break?' he found himself asking, before the thought had even fully formed in his brain. Her brown eyes visibly widening in surprise, he heard her release a long slow breath.

'If I can spare the time…why?'

Why, indeed? Jack was asking himself as he listened in on his own suggestion with increasing incredulity at the lack of wisdom it contained. *Just what in God's name did he think he was doing by making it clear that he wanted to see her again?* He scrubbed his hand round his jaw, as if he was all but contemplating flying a plane and then turning off the engine mid-flight and letting himself plummet to the ground, to crash, burn and die.

'I don't think I have an answer for that right now… do *you?*'

Trapped in a hypnotic spell that suddenly seemed to make the world stand still, Caroline stared back at him with equal confusion…equal knowledge that in the world of right-thinking decisions this one wouldn't even get its *toe* in the door.

'No…no, I don't.'

'One o'clock okay with you?'

A little shudder of heat rippled through her. 'That's fine.'

'See you then.'

Before either of them could come to their senses and fully realise the sheer stupidity of such an arrangement Jack quickly walked away in the opposite direction, and didn't once glance back…

Nicholas rang. He told her he had something important that he wanted to discuss. Fearful that he might be going to reiterate his warning to her about Jack, Caroline found she wasn't looking forward to the prospect.

Having agreed that he could drop round that evening to see her, she tried to focus on work. But—between serving customers and trying to put her piling paperwork into some kind of helpful order—her thoughts inevitably returned to Jack, and that promise of his to stop by at lunchtime…

The shop was empty, and there was a sign on the door that read 'Closed for Lunch'. Not entirely certain that Caroline hadn't decided to go out for lunch and stand him up, Jack hesitated for a long moment before pressing the bell at the side of the door. If she was out, he told himself, she would be doing them *both* a huge favour. One of them should come to their senses and put an end to this…this *suicide* mission.

But, even though he prayed she *would* be out, so he could walk away from her relatively *unscathed*, Jack knew that it was already too late. From the moment he'd bumped into her the other day, and they had stood face to face after a lapse of time that should have permanently erased all want, need, or desire for ever, Jack had known that trying to resist Caroline Tremayne was like trying to resist a life-saving drink of water when you'd been stumbling through the desert for days without one. He was fatally infatuated by her…always had been and probably always *would* be. *It was an infatuation that was surely destined to bring them both nothing but further agony of spirit.*

He pressed the bell.

'Come in.'

Jack both cursed and thanked God at the same time for her almost immediate appearance.

Watching him warily from beneath her dark blonde lashes, worrying that she had answered the bell too quickly and might appear over eager to see him, Caroline stood back to let Jack enter. Once inside the colourful interior of the shop, she carefully shut the door again, and turned the latch. Glancing up guiltily as he watched her perform this action, she witnessed the merest glimmer of a mocking smile touch the corners of his mouth.

'If I don't lock the door we won't get any peace

while we're eating,' she remarked nervously, endeavouring to keep her voice light.

Pulling the knitted edges of her long dove-grey cardigan closer together, so that they overlapped the plain black sweatshirt and jeans she wore underneath, Caroline was glad she had donned these nondescript items of clothing, because they lent her psychological protection against the man who was currently putting her so helplessly on edge. She would not have him imagine for even a second that she was hoping to appear alluring or appealing in any way, to resurrect potentially hazardous long-dead feelings between them. All she planned for them to do was eat the sandwiches she had bought from the bakers, have a cup of tea, and keep the conversation as neutral as possible—because they were both mature adults…and then Jack would leave.

But when she glanced across the room, and her anxious searching gaze fell beneath the spell of his dangerously irresistible blue eyes, Caroline knew with devastating certainty that the supposedly 'long-dead' feelings they had once passionately felt for each other still simmered perilously close to the surface, and weren't going to go away any time soon. *Surely she'd been mad to think that they might do something as ordinarily mundane as share some sandwiches and tea together, as though they were two old friends catching up on old times?* Especially when the Jack Fitzgerald who stood before her today had the kind of imposing presence that was hardly conducive to relaxation of any sort. Everything about his expensively groomed appearance quite frankly put him completely out of Caroline's league. He was a far cry from the wild passionate boy who'd willingly shared his dreams with her, who she had fallen in love with so long ago...

'We'll go into the back room, if you like,' she said breezily, sweeping past him. 'I usually eat my lunch there. I've got the kettle on and I—'

Before she got any further Jack swung her round, captured her head between his hands and kissed her ruthlessly on the mouth. When she drew back, stunned, his hands slid down from her face onto her shoulders, and Caroline was immediately aware that he intended to keep her right where she was until he decided different. His nostrils flared a little as he swept her with a heated, ardent stare, and such a feeling of hunger raged through her blood that she wondered how she didn't immediately succumb to it—completely abandon all common sense and caution and simply let the most basic of primal longings have its way.

'What is this...this *hold* you seem to have on me, Caroline?' he asked gruffly, the palpable tension he exuded holding her spellbound.

Her mouth aching from his avidly voracious assault on her lips, Caroline barely knew how to answer him. His words had astonished her, because the very *idea* of her having any kind of hold on such a man seemed completely *preposterous*. He was angry with her, that was all. Still furious because she'd had an abortion instead of going through with the pregnancy. Anger could easily spill over into passion, and Caroline knew with certainty that that was *all* this was about. There'd been no mellowing towards her over the years, and certainly no forgiveness now that Jack had seen her again. *Did she dislike herself so much that she'd willingly let him walk in here and treat her with such demoralising disrespect?*

'I don't have any kind of "hold" over you, Jack. It's all in your imagination. I didn't *ask* you to come back here. I've just been minding my own business and getting on with my life, never once looking to contact you or see you again. Do you know how upsetting it is for me to have you walk in here and kiss me like you just kissed me? As if—as if I still *owe* you something? I think it's probably best if you just go. Having lunch together was an *insane* idea.'

Hearing her words, Jack didn't dispute the sense in them. Yet still he lingered, still his fingers bit possessively into her slender shoulders, as if waiting for some kind of divine inspiration that would tell him what to do about this—this *compulsion* he had for this woman.

Thinking about her accusation, he couldn't deny that he *did* have a sense of Caroline 'owing' him. She'd dispensed with their unborn child as though the decision were hers and hers alone…as if he'd had *no rights and no say* in the matter whatsoever. According to her father, only people from *their* class had those kind of rights. That thought alone had kept his animosity towards her simmering beneath the outward show of his material and professional success all this time.

Releasing his grip, he stood back and breathed in deeply through his nostrils. He thought about all that had happened in those intervening years since he'd left Caroline. First travelling to the States, working and studying at the same time, to gain an understanding of the world of finance, putting his cast-iron determination to good use in helping him rise above his difficult beginnings and make money…a *lot* of money…so that he would never be poor again, *never* be shown the door by anyone who imagined themselves better than he was ever again.

And, besides the money that had started to rain down on him in ever-increasing abundance, there had been *other* compensations too. There had been the undoubted admiration from the financial world in which he worked—the 'movers and shakers' in that world often holding their breath as they watched him accomplish success after success, until eventually he usurped theirs. And there had been the accumulation of beautiful homes—in New York, California and Connecticut, and lately Paris. He'd just signed the lease on a fantastic penthouse apartment in the heart of that lovely city.

Then, of course, there had also been the *women*. Over the years Jack had dated models, actresses, socialites, and women who were as ambitious in their careers as he was. He'd had some good times, some reasonably exciting sex, and led the life of a highly ambitious, successful and *rich* man about town. *But no woman had really touched his heart since his youthful passion for Caroline Tremayne.* Not even Anna—the stunning ballerina from the Russian ballet whom he had met and married after a surprisingly swift courtship just three years ago, and to whom he had vowed he would stay faithful even if he didn't—*couldn't*—love her as she deserved. When he'd discovered that she was having an affair with the interior designer he'd hired to redesign their Manhattan apartment Jack had felt deflated, resigned, but *not* devastated by her betrayal. How could he when he had known where the fault *really* lay? It wasn't necessary now, at Jack's level of success, to put in the working hours that he did, and he *certainly* didn't need any more money than he had already, but any woman would eventually become frustrated by a husband who was never home.

And then had come the heart attack. Thinking of it now, Jack automatically laid his hand against his chest and winced, wishing he could demolish the fear that gripped him for good. Seeing the slight drawing together of Caroline's dark brows—a frown that might spell concern—he quickly moved his hand away and shrugged.

'Why didn't you ever marry?' he found himself asking.

Snapping out of the spell she had fallen under, Caroline felt her fingers clench a little round the edges of her wool cardigan. 'I wasn't aware that getting married was on the statute books,' she answered a little coolly.

'It must have disappointed your father that you didn't

wed,' Jack remarked. 'No high-powered and ambitious son-in-law from the right class to welcome into the fold?'

Hearing the undoubted bitterness in his tone, Caroline shivered. 'Did you ask that question just so that you could have another pop at my father? What's the point, Jack? He's long dead.'

Turning away from him, Caroline moved towards the door she'd just locked and unlocked it. Clearly upset, she opened it and carelessly brushed back a pale frond of golden hair from the side of her cheek.

The gesture made her appear far too vulnerable for Jack's liking, and he deliberately stayed where he was... *almost* but not quite despising himself for his next question. A question that had troubled him often over the years and caused him many a 'dark night of the soul'.

'Did it make your life any *easier*, going through with the abortion?'

Witnessing the convulsive swallow in her throat, and the immediate sheen of tears covering her liquid dark eyes, Jack decided he *did* despise himself after all...

'Get out.'

There was no fury in her voice, just a quiet dignity and a deep, abiding sense of heartbreak that cut Jack to the quick and made him feel like an utter bastard. Unable to do anything but regard her with equal parts longing, regret and rage swirling inside him, Jack nodded his head—as if in complete agreement with her decision for him to go—and swept past her without saying another word...

* * *

'What happened to your lip?'

Before she could duck away, Nicholas had tilted Caroline's chin towards him and examined the slight swelling at the right-hand corner of her lip with a concerned and at the same time professional eye.

'I—I must have inadvertently bit it, or something...I don't know. It's hardly important.'

Pulling away, Caroline tempered her irritable response to Nicholas's concern with an apologetic smile. She too had been slightly shocked to see the damning evidence of Jack's furious kiss when she'd seen it reflected back at her in the bathroom mirror. She certainly didn't want to tell her friend the truth about the cause of her tender abrasion. He'd already warned her against seeing Jack again, and she had ignored his advice and visited nothing but heartache on herself once more.

How could Jack believe for one moment that her life could possibly have been made easier because she'd had an abortion? Caroline wanted to die every time she recalled him asking that wickedly cruel question. But she expressly didn't want to discuss Jack Fitzgerald this evening and make herself feel even more blue. She really hoped that that particular subject was *not* on Nicholas's agenda.

Shaking off the gloom that kept clutching at her heart, she decided to try and keep the conversation as light as possible. 'Will you have a glass of wine?'

Moving across the room, Caroline lifted the bottle of

Châteauneuf-du-Pape she'd left on the tray next to two sparkling wine glasses.

Settling himself into the studded Chesterfield-style armchair by the fire, Nicholas smiled warmly in agreement. 'That would be lovely, darling…thank you.'

Thinking how at home he appeared, sitting there by the crackling open fire on this chilly almost winter evening, in what had been her father's favourite chair, Caroline wondered why, for the first time ever, she wished he *didn't* make himself look so at home there. Telling herself it was because she was still feeling on edge and unhappy from yet another upsetting encounter with Jack, she dismissed her slight feeling of unease and poured out the wine.

Handing a glass to Nicholas, she lowered herself into the fawn-coloured chair opposite and took a sip of her own drink. The alcohol immediately warming her, Caroline told herself that everything was going to be all right…that there was no need for her to be worried about anything.

'So…what was it you wanted to talk to me about?' she asked, leaning forward in her chair.

Nicholas took a sip of his wine, savoured it for a moment, then regarded Caroline with a deepening of the kindly smile she had long grown used to.

'I suppose I may as well get straight to the point.' Still smiling, Nicholas leant back in his chair with a relaxed sigh. 'I wanted to talk to you about something that has been on my mind for quite some time now.'

'Oh? What's that?' Caroline gulped a little too much wine and felt the alcohol hurtle through her veins with fierce heat.

'It's a *personal* matter, actually,' Nicholas replied.

When she didn't immediately comment, he frowned.

'Shall I go on?' he asked.

Caroline wanted to say no. She was all of a sudden very tired, as well as feeling emotionally bruised, and she wanted to say she had a headache and didn't feel up to spending the evening with him after all. But good manners and gratitude for the man's friendship to both her father *and* herself prevented her from going with her natural instincts.

'Of course…please, do go on.'

'We've known each other for a long time, haven't we?' Briefly tapping his wine glass with his fingernails, Nicholas stopped the action almost immediately he realised he was doing it—as if inadvertently revealing a displeasing character trait he'd much rather keep hidden.

Watching him, Caroline was surprised by the tension in him that she'd immediately picked up. For some inexplicable reason a sense of acute alarm arose inside her. His question not really requiring a reply, she nodded her assent instead.

'It was hard losing Meg after being married for so many years…I can't begin to tell you how hard. I've discovered that I'm not a man who likes being alone, Caroline. I need conversation, stimulus, after a long day's work, and Meg was always there for me…come rain or shine. A man gets used to that kind of care from the woman in his life. Anyway, at the risk of making myself sound too foolish…I have decided that I would rather not be on my own any longer.'

CHAPTER SEVEN

HE WASN'T… He couldn't be going to ask her to—

Sitting straight-backed in her chair, Caroline stared hard at Nicholas, almost willing him to change his mind and not say another word on the topic that was clearly presenting him *and now her* with such unease. Besides…it was too ridiculous, too preposterous to even—

'I'd like us to become engaged to be married—if that's acceptable to you, Caroline?' Nicholas pressed on, reaching up to his shirt collar to pull it slightly away from his neck, where it had suddenly clearly become uncomfortably tight.

Oh God… He was… Leaving her wine glass on the coffee table between them, Caroline got up from her chair and put her hands together, almost though unconsciously praying. The heat from the fire feeling suddenly more akin to the heat from a roaring bonfire, she tried to smile at the man waiting patiently in her father's old chair for her reaction.

'Engaged Nicholas? You and I? Are you serious?'

'Perfectly!'

'But it's—this is such a shock!'

'A pleasant one, I hope?'

He didn't rise from the chair, as Caroline had half expected him to. Instead he regarded her from it, as though his greater age and experience, his profession, dictated he had the right.

She tried to imagine being married to this man she had long regarded as a family friend. Apart from the age difference, which wouldn't have been an issue at all if she had been in love with him, she knew no matter how desperately alone she felt at times she could not, *would* not, simply marry a man to fill the void left by the death of his wife—*or* because she might end up on her own if she didn't. Nicholas didn't love her either. He might genuinely be fond of her, Caroline mused, but all he really wanted was a companion and housekeeper—someone to be there to listen to the events of his day, someone to cook for him and clean his house, and, yes…someone to pour him a glass of good red wine while he sat by the fire on a cold winter's evening.

And when she thought about going to bed with him… Caroline felt herself grow alternately hot then cold with embarrassment. She'd known this man since she was a teenager. At her father's behest she had looked upon him as a kind of 'uncle'. But—more pertinent than that—how could she even contemplate sharing the intimacies of marriage with a man she neither loved *nor* desired? And especially after becoming so shockingly reacquainted with the *one* man she'd given her heart to so long ago?

Without really meaning to, she found herself touching the slightly raised area on her lip where Jack had kissed her so bitterly and yet with such undeniable need earlier today, and was taken aback by the inescapable rush of pleasure that suddenly throbbed like molten lava through her veins. Immediately Caroline dropped her hand, silently scolding herself for dwelling on the memory of his lustfully hot kiss instead of that cruel question he'd asked, which had wounded her almost too deeply for tears.

'I—I know how much you loved Meg…how much she meant to you. How can I be anything but tremendously flattered that you would even consider asking me to get engaged to you, Nicholas?'

Hugging her arms across her chest, Caroline knew her awkward smile was concerned, but regretful. She didn't want to hurt Nicholas, or make him feel bad in any way, and she certainly didn't want to lose his very dear and valuable friendship but she had to make him see that a more personal relationship, was definitely *not* on the agenda.

'But the truth is,' she continued, 'I'd much rather keep our friendship than potentially spoil what we have by trying to turn our relationship into something it *isn't*.'

This time Nicholas *did* get to his feet. Putting his wine aside, he captured the ends of Caroline's fingers in his own and brushed over them with the pads of his thumbs. It was true that there was tenderness in his expression as he gazed at her, but against the fiery, electrically-charged glances that Jack cast her it was like comparing ice-cubes to burning hot coals…

'Why assume our getting engaged and then married would spoil our friendship…hmm?' Releasing one of her hands, he brushed aside a radiant curl of shining gold that had glanced against her smooth forehead. 'The strongest unions are *always* the ones that start out with friendship. It was certainly that way for Meg and me. We have a great *bond*, Caroline. I admire you and like you more than I could begin to say. I can't think of anyone I would like more to be my wife than you. At least think about it, will you? I wasn't expecting a decision straight away…'

'I'm sorry, Nicholas, but I don't really need any time to think about it. I know it can't have been easy for you to broach the subject…and it's a terrific compliment to be asked…but I'm afraid my answer *has* to be no.'

Not liking the sudden sense of intimacy he was forcing upon her that was so at odds with all these years of steady platonic friendship, Caroline drew away from his near embrace and moved across the room to the door that stood ajar.

'I think I'm going to make a cup of tea…would you like one?'

Genuinely perplexed, Nicholas shook his head. 'No, thank you. I don't think I *would* like a cup of tea right now. If I've offended you in any way, Caroline, let me be the first to assure you that I—'

Suddenly wishing that he would go, Caroline felt as

though she might explode with the tension that had gathered force inside her. So many emotions were charging through her all at once that she scarcely knew what to do with them. *She didn't want to marry Nicholas— her father's closest friend.* She didn't want to sacrifice herself for *any* man—no matter what the reason—*ever* again. And she certainly didn't want to spend another seventeen years heartsore and racked with too much guilt over a man who barely even accorded her the *right* to possess hurt feelings because he was so certain that *he* was the one who had been so cruelly wronged. She would not be pushed into a corner again by anybody!

'You haven't offended me at all, Nicholas, but I really don't want to discuss this any further. I just—I'm sorry, but I really need to be by myself right now. Please try and understand.'

Straightening the cuffs on his shirtsleeves beneath his very conservative tweed sports jacket, Nicholas patted down his pockets distractedly as he walked towards her, clearly both embarrassed and confused by Caroline's rejection of his proposal—a response he obviously had not been expecting.

'I certainly wouldn't dream of outstaying my welcome, Caroline. We'd best just leave things as they stand for a day or two, under the circumstances, and then I'll ring you. That all right with you?'

Unable to bring herself to look at him directly, Caroline nodded mutely.

* * *

Feeling the need to escape for a while, Jack had driven to London, booked into a small chic hotel in Chelsea owned by an American friend, then called up that same friend's sister, whom he'd briefly dated before meeting Anna and who was now based in the UK, working for an insurance company in the city.

Amanda Morton was a woman of the world—she'd understand that Jack wasn't calling her to renew their relationship but was simply looking for a little female company while he was in town. They'd parted on amicable terms, remained friends, and Jack was merely fulfilling a promise that if he was ever in London he'd look her up.

Now, as he sat next to her in the low-lit bar area in the luxurious lounge of a famous hotel, her slender thigh pressed up close to his as she regaled him with gossip from her office as though any higher concerns—such as life, death and the universe—never even entered her brain, Jack remembered why his relationship with Amanda had not progressed much beyond two or three dates. Certainly her looks couldn't be faulted, with her elegantly styled blonde hair, slender figure and sparkly blue eyes, but Jack couldn't help thinking of another blonde—one with delectable *brown* eyes—who he'd last seen wearing an expression of inconsolable sadness and hurt…*put there by him.*

About to take a deep slug of the bourbon on the rocks that he had ordered, Jack shifted in his seat, put down his glass, and came to a decision that surprised even himself.

Amanda immediately stopped talking and cast him

a highly flirtatious glance from beneath her heavily mascaraed lashes.

'What's up, sweetie? Don't you like it here? We can go someplace else if you'd like?'

'I'm sorry, Amanda, but I have to go.'

'Go?'

She blinked up at him in bewilderment as he rose to his full six feet two inches. His handsome face was preoccupied and his mouth drawn—immediately alerting even the oblivious Amanda to the fact that his mind had not been as attentive to her conversation as she might have liked.

'What do you mean, you have to go? We've barely just got here!' she declared in dismay. 'I know you're not interested in seeing me on a regular basis, Jack, but I'd at least hoped we'd wind up in bed together before the night was through!'

Why had he done it? Jack asked himself. Why had he called up a woman he'd barely been able to muster the most fleeting interest in when he'd first stupidly dated her and expected her to help distract him from the unpalatable turmoil that had assailed him since he'd left Caroline back home with that stricken look in her eyes? All he knew right then was that his need to see the girl the youthful Jack Fitzgerald had fallen in love with was impossible to ignore, and his thoughts and feelings would give him no peace—even if he jumped on a plane to Alaska to escape them—if he didn't drive straight back to her right now. It didn't matter that his inexplicable desire had no rhyme or reason, or that the outcome of it would probably result in even *more*, unwelcome turmoil than he was enduring already, he simply had to go back and see her.

'I'm sorry, Amanda.'

Employing full mercenary use of his undoubted charisma, Jack tipped up Amanda's chin and smiled beguilingly into her eyes as she stood up and seductively leaned towards him. Her perfume was a little on the overpowering side, and Jack fleetingly wondered why some women never understood the power of subtlety, no matter if they came from money or not. Money couldn't buy class, and that was a fact.

The thought immediately made Jack think of Caroline, and he couldn't help but silently admit that she had always had that commodity in abundance...*even* when she was only seventeen. And it wasn't just social class he was thinking about either. Her grace, beauty and innocence had made Jack feel like a much better man than he knew himself to be whenever he'd been around her.

'I don't mean any insult, but it was wrong of me to call you when I had other things on my mind that need taking care of. Things that I now realise I simply *can't* leave unattended. Can you forgive me?'

'It depends what "other things" are on your mind, Jack,' Amanda crooned softly, winding his silk tie round her fingers and tugging on it a little. 'If it's work...well, being ambitious for my own career, I can totally understand such a preoccupation. But on the other hand...if

it's another *woman* that's been distracting your mind…
then I might, just *might*, be a teensy-weensy bit upset
about that.'

Feeling his patience getting a little strained, Jack
abruptly rescued his tie and kissed the pouting Amanda
as briefly as possible on her forehead. Pressing some
notes from his wallet into her hand, he smiled. 'Get
yourself a cab home. I won't forget I owe you dinner,'
he declared as he turned to walk across the hotel lounge.

And tomorrow he would send her the biggest
bouquet he could order from the florists to make up for
the disappointment of his desertion tonight. But even as
he ventured one last glance round, as he reached the
twin doors that led into the lobby, he smiled wryly to
himself as he saw Amanda walk confidently up to the
bar and start avidly chatting to the young, good-looking Spanish bartender behind it…

Caroline had driven to the beach after Nicholas had left,
and walked the length of the sandy cove with the rain
and wind lashing at her clothing and stinging her face.
She'd cried, secure in the knowledge that nobody else
would witness her descent into misery, that only someone desperate of spirit would be out walking along a
deserted beach in the dark with the rain bucketing down
as though God was emptying out a heavenly reservoir
upon her head.

She'd desperately needed the release of tears, and
after Nicholas's unexpected and, it had to be said, un-

welcome proposal she knew the tide of change that was rolling towards her was both inevitable and unstoppable. After this, she could rely on nothing to stay the same. Even her good memories of Jack would be tainted by his reappearance, and the churning-up of emotions that his presence had cruelly revisited upon her. Caroline had sobbed desperately for the predicament she found herself in—for the unimaginably traumatic sense of loss and grief that she had suffered through having the abortion and then being shunned by her baby's father, the man she had loved *beyond* imagining, the man who was never, *ever* going to either understand or forgive her for what she had done…

By the time she got back to the house she was thoroughly drenched, and shivering with cold, and she immediately went upstairs, stripped off, donned her warm dressing-gown and ran a hot bath. Half an hour later, once again ensconced in the old-fashioned comfort of her dressing-gown, her feet up on her armchair's matching footstool as she sipped a mug of hot cinnamon-flavoured milk in front of the fire, Caroline silently and thankfully acknowledged that her misery had ebbed a little and the heat and comfort of her home were helping subdue some of the tremendous hurt that had deluged her.

The only way forward, she concluded, thinking hard as she stared into the flames flickering in the grate, was to somehow learn to forgive herself for what she'd done…*and also forgive Jack for blaming her.* That was the only way she could really put the past behind her and look forward to a happier future. Maybe she should re-examine the possibility of earning her living as an artist? It wasn't too late. And she could still teach part-time, as she was doing, and give encouragement and the benefit of her experience to young girls like Sadie Martin. Change shouldn't be feared.

If Nicholas couldn't remain the friend he'd always been she still had other friends she could count on…and she would make new ones too. But at the same time she couldn't keep looking *outside* for the source of her happiness…it simply *had* to come from within, or else she'd for ever be at the mercy of external forces. When she next saw Jack…*if* she saw him again…and her pulse raced a little at the idea she might not…Caroline was determined to tell him about the decision she had reached. He could continue to blame her for as long as he liked, but he would have to understand that she was no longer going to be a willing victim of that blame. She was steering the ship of her own life and would not let anyone knock her off course again, no matter *who* they were.

Having finished her drink, Caroline put down her mug and snuggled up into the chair with her feet drawn up beneath her. Continuing to stare into the hypnotic flames that danced across the coals in the grate, before she knew it sleep had seductively beckoned.

Into her dreams intruded the incongruous chimes of the doorbell. Jolting upright with shock, Caroline opened her eyes wide and glanced frantically up at the clock on the mantel. It was almost half-past one in the morning…hardly a sensible time for callers of any description…so who could it be?

Uncurling her legs from beneath her, and rising anxiously, she yelped in pain when the arch of her foot almost bent double with cramp. Falling back into the chair, she quickly rubbed at the offending area, praying that the doorbell would not chime again—hoping that whoever it was who had rung it had mistakenly stopped outside the wrong door and had now realised his or her mistake and moved on. *No such luck.* As the echo of the ringing chimes demonstrated her caller's persistence, Caroline got slowly to her feet, her cramp now gone and her skin clammily cold with fright.

Glancing at the iron poker in the brass stand beside the grate, she did seriously wonder about taking it with her—but then an obstinate refusal to believe that she wasn't safe in her own home suddenly collared her fear by the throat and sent her striding confidently out to the front door…*without* the poker.

When she saw the definite shadow of a man's figure outside the stained glass panels in the door, Caroline almost breathed a sigh of relief, thinking it must be Nicholas. He'd probably been called out to see a patient and, driving home again, had seen some of her house lights on because she had fallen asleep in the chair and hadn't turned them out yet. Hoping that he didn't hold a grudge against her because she'd earlier refused his request to get engaged, Caroline undid the locks and pulled open the door.

'Jack!'

Her legs trembled hard at the sight of her ex-lover. Grasping the fleece lapels of her robe together in her hand across her chest, Caroline simply stared at him as he shrugged inside his raincoat, his dark hair sheened by the rain and the starkly defined planes and angles of his amazing face disturbingly highlighted by the illumination from inside the house.

'What is it? Has something happened?'

She had the most unnatural feeling that she was speaking in slow motion. But, even though Jack's appearance was a total mystery and a shock to her, something inside Caroline couldn't help but foolishly grasp at the most impossible hope.

'I needed to see you. I realise it's very late, but can I come in?'

As logic briefly superseded her impossible hope, she wanted to say no. This man was like a broken arrow embedded in her heart. Inviting him over her threshold would be like inviting him to deepen that wound even more. Already her throat was constricting with anguish at the sight of him.

In the end, because words simply deserted her, Caroline just watched with a mounting sense of unreality as Jack came inside, shucked off his raincoat, hung it on the coatstand, then came back to her—his ardent gaze studying her in a way that made her bones turn to liquid silk. Without saying a word he cupped the side of her face with his hand, the startling touch of his cool skin acquainting her with the chill of the rainy night outside. He kept his palm there with a gentleness that ripped the breath from Caroline's lungs. As her wary and captivated gaze examined the arresting features and sharply drawn jawline before her—that jawline denoted he was wilful as well as meeting life on his own terms, with little regard for anyone else's *modus operandi*— she found herself wondering if they would still be together now if she hadn't fallen pregnant and her father hadn't made her have a termination. God knew she'd been crazy about him…crazy enough to jump ship and elope with him to the States or anywhere else he suggested if he had but asked. *He never had.*

She knew this was dangerous thinking. What Jack was doing here in the middle of the night she had no idea, but one thing Caroline *was* certain of—she wasn't going to let him make her feel bad about herself ever again.

She broke free of his touch, unconsciously pursing her dry lips to moisten them as he watched her, his brooding gaze still cleaving to her face as though he couldn't bear to look anywhere else but at *her.*

'What do you want, Jack?'

'Isn't that obvious?'

'I wouldn't have asked if I didn't—'

'You,' he came back, before she'd even finished the sentence, his lips unsmiling and for once without mockery.

A high-voltage charge of heat bolted through

Caroline's middle, making her hips soft and the rest of her body feel as if she could climb out of her very skin with the seductive promise his disturbing reply created.

'That's a very bad joke, under the circumstances,' she returned huskily, feeling as if she really was losing her hold on reality. 'I think you'd better just go.'

'What if I don't want to?' Jack asked, moving purposefully towards her even as he registered the distress on her face. 'What if…deep down…you don't *want* me to go either, Caroline?'

CHAPTER EIGHT

'You must be delusional!' Her dark eyes flashed her indignant denial even as, terrifyingly, she registered his hand sliding expertly behind her neck beneath the soft tousled fall of her hair, and his mouth moving threateningly closer to hers. 'I don't want you to stay…I want you to go! Do you think I *enjoy* being hurt by you? When I saw you last you left me under no illusion as to what you thought of me and your words cut me in two! What we had was finished a long time ago, Jack. Why not just accept that and walk away now? Just forget me and go!'

Jack was struck by the ragged truth of Caroline's impassioned words. He *should* just walk away and forget her, as she'd advised, and spare them both further agony. But even as his lips stilled, scant inches from hers, he knew that trying to curtail his increasing desire for her was like hoping to douse an inferno with a mere thimbleful of water. His senses were held in thrall by her.

In the gently dimmed light that flooded out into the hall from the living room, she looked like the impossibly beautiful heroine from a fairy tale. Her dark gaze was sleepily soft, even though her eyes danced with anger, and her hair felt like gossamer as it glanced against the back of his hand. God help him, but Jack had dreamed of holding her like this so many times over the years! But then usually, after he'd surrendered to the impulse to think about Caroline, he'd be infused with agonising hurt about her having the abortion and betraying both him *and* their unborn child. He'd *hate* her then, and the impulse—the tormenting, feverish longing to recall how she had felt in his arms—would abruptly leave him.

But right now it wasn't hatred that was dominating Jack's senses but a ravenous, almost obsessive compulsion to know her again in the most libidinous and intimate way. Everything about her put him under a spell of longing.

'I know what we had is long over,' he intonated throatily, his compelling blue irises darkening as he stared into Caroline's startled gaze. 'But what if—what if I asked you to share just one more night with me? What then, Caroline? Would you turn me away out into the rain again when right now I need to hold you more than anything else I need in this entire world?'

He didn't play fair. He found her most vulnerable spot and ruthlessly exploited it. Right from that very first moment, when he'd arrested her curious, aroused gaze with his lazy and bold examination of her when she was with her schoolfriends, Jack had assumed an early and definitely *powerful* advantage over Caroline's captivated senses. Now she was once again besieged by his blatantly sensual masculinity, and the incessant throbbing yearning that surged through her heart at his seductive words made her realise that she was too weak to deny him…to deny *herself*.

Feeling herself sway, all the strength in her legs seemed to treacherously desert her as Jack caught her feverishly in his arms and with devastating thoroughness laid voracious claim to her lips. Drenching heat and exquisitely male flavours burst over her mouth, and Caroline heard herself making small betraying sounds of shameless longing. Jack swept her mouth with his tongue, stroking and teasing hers with unbelievably erotic torment as he gathered a fistful of her soft silken hair in his hand and massaged her scalp with his fingers. His lean hips increased the torment he was delivering as he pressed them demandingly into hers, hinting at a wild white-water ride of incalculable pleasure and rediscovery that made Caroline breathless.

'Jack…'

Every ounce of longing she had in her entire being was in the soft, heartfelt whisper of his name. She had lost so much…her baby *and* Jack… How could she pass up the chance for them to be together again for even a short while, she asked herself desperately, when she ached so hard for him that it was *unthinkable* to ask him to leave?

'Have mercy,' he replied, his warm breath caressing the side of her neck, closely followed by his lips. 'Please don't tell me you've changed your mind… I want you so badly I'm shaking. Can you feel it?'

She could. Although there was humour in his wry remark, there was an underlying fear and desperation there too. Extricating herself firmly from his ardent embrace, Caroline swept back her dishevelled golden hair with her fingers and glanced nervously towards the open door that led into the living room.

'There's a fire…it needs—it needs building up, but the embers are still burning.' *She could have been talking about their relationship and the irony was not lost on her.*

Jack's piercing gaze examined her for so long that Caroline momentarily feared that *he* was the one who had changed his mind about making love to *her.* Glancing anxiously away, she felt her breath catch in her throat when he suddenly moved closer and slipped his arm possessively around her waist, bestowing a smile so dangerously beguiling that she was reminded of the eager, devil-may-care, youthful Jack—who had so determinedly and doggedly pursued her in spite of the dire warnings and threats from Caroline's father. There was a big part of her that still grieved for the innocent passion they had lost so cruelly…

He made up the fire again while Caroline watched, silently begging him to finish quickly and join her again. When he did, he drew her down to the patterned colourful rug, with its tones of burnished copper and warm reds, that adorned the space in front of the fire. Then, lifting his dark green lambswool sweater over his head, he carelessly discarded it before slowly undoing the tie-belt of Caroline's dressing-gown that was fastened around her small hourglass waist.

She couldn't stop shivering as his hands first touched her clothing, then her skin—his intensely blue eyes making her a slave to his increasingly heated glance. When she did manage to tear her gaze free, it was only for it to linger on the taut, well-formed display of muscle at the tops of his arms, so temptingly revealed by his fitted T-shirt.

A hot, melting flurry of acute awareness dispersed through Caroline's insides when she saw the dark tattoo of a raven carved into his left bicep. He must have acquired it after he had left her, she realized, curious as to what it was supposed to symbolise. *And there was no doubt in her mind that it meant something.* Something that very few people would know outright. That was one of the things about Jack that had been such a magnet for Caroline. *He'd always been almost frighteningly inscrutable and unpredictable—had always left her with the sense that he knew things about life that no one else knew...*

'Let's take this off, shall we?'

Relieving her of her dressing-gown, Jack directed his attention to the perfectly beautiful delineation of her slender shoulders in the flimsily strapped white cotton nightgown, to the temptingly bountiful swell of her full breasts and the noticeable imprint of her puckered nipples behind the pristine cotton. With her hair tumbling and curling like golden flame down her back, highlighted by the vivid colours reflected from the fire, her expression was focused totally on him and entirely serious. *Jack guessed how King Solomon must have felt when the Queen of Sheba had revealed herself to him from a rolled-up carpet.* Her incandescent beauty stunned him.

A powerful memory surfaced inside Jack from long ago, when they had made love for the very first time. Her loveliness had left him dry-mouthed in awe then too.

The venue for the occasion had been a cheap hotel on the outskirts of town where no one would know them, and when Jack had eagerly helped Caroline undress he had finally seen her the way he'd been hungering to see her since the day they'd met. She'd been the most breathtakingly beautiful girl he'd ever set eyes on, and she had wanted to be with him—not some 'upper class aspiring doctor' that her father picked out for her. That very gratifying realisation alone had helped cement Jack's already strong feelings for her. His spirits had soared to the sky at the knowledge that she wanted to share her beautiful body with *him…that he was going to be her very first lover and, if Jack had his way, her only lover.*

Now the denial of that fervent wish twisted his heart with unbelievable hurt. To imagine her giving herself in that way to somebody else… *Caroline was his.*

Faced with the extraordinarily jealous urge that swept him, Jack could no longer pretend even to himself that his possessive feelings towards her had grown less passionate or intense throughout all the years of separation.

'What's this?' With a shy smile that caught him completely off guard, Caroline gently touched the outline of his tattoo.

Capturing her slender, fine-boned wrist between his fingers, Jack made a gruff noise in his throat, then smiled. 'It's a raven. The Native Americans believe that it has the power to shape-shift—to move from one dimension to another. It can also symbolise visiting the darker parts of your soul.'

She detected the minutest flicker of a shadow in his fascinating blue eyes that left her in no doubt that he was well acquainted with the darker parts of his own soul.

Shivering as he raised her hand to his lips and gently kissed it, Caroline longed to be able to convey to him how desperately she regretted perpetrating the act that had finally forced them apart. In that moment she realised that Jack was still harbouring a wealth of animosity and pain in his soul because of her. And, although she definitely intended to let him know that she was no longer going to be a willing victim of that animosity and pain—no matter *how* regretful she was—Caroline also experienced an overwhelming urge to demonstrate to him her intense sadness that their love had been dashed to the rocks and splintered for ever…

'I've done that too, Jack,' she whispered, studying him intently. 'Visited the darker part of my soul. But despising what I found there didn't help me. We have to learn to forgive, don't we? I mean…even ourselves. Then we can move on and hopefully make something of our lives. I'm so sorry about what happened between us. If I could turn back time and undo all the dreadful hurt I would.'

Learn to forgive? For a moment his jaw tightened with overwhelming emotion. Jack didn't know if he would *ever* be able to do that. Because of what Caroline had done, he had not sought to father another child with a woman. He had been far too fearful of a repetition of the past. But—deep in the far reaches of his soul—Jack still *longed* to experience fatherhood. Else what had all his hard work and driving ambition been *for?* Having a child of his own would help make up for every excruciating splinter of hurt that his own disastrous family life had driven into his heart…

'I think you've grown even more lovely over the years.' Deliberately diverting the conversation from things that were too painful to reflect upon, Jack kissed Caroline softly on the mouth, contact with her moist, sultry lips fuelling his desire once more into restless burning flame.

How could she do anything *other* than dissolve in his arms at such a heartwarming statement? Even though she was crushingly disappointed that he hadn't responded positively to her suggestion of forgiveness, Caroline nonetheless couldn't deny the increasingly restless need that was building inexorably inside her body at Jack's closeness.

His kiss deepened devastatingly. The pleasure it wrought inside her took Caroline to such heights of unimaginable joy that she knew that when Jack was long gone she would remember the intensity of those feelings for the rest of her life.

Feeling his hands drop to her shoulders to guide her gently onto the rug beneath them, she watched him undress—her mind registering his undoubted masculine perfection with growing anticipation, seeing for herself that her girlhood lover had definitely turned into the most awesome man. Yanking his T-shirt over his dark head, Jack let it drop where it fell. Then, kneeling down, he joined Caroline on the rug.

As he bent towards her, she was taken aback by the slender ridged scar she saw on his chest. Glancing up into his unfathomable blue eyes, she felt her stomach tighten as a bump of fear pulsed through it. If he saw that she was curious, Jack chose to ignore it. Instead his warm breath fanned across her mouth as he lowered his head to kiss her again.

'What happened? How did you get this?'

Her words interrupted his all too clear intention. As the firelight flickered across her illuminated and concerned features, Jack silently cursed. 'It's nothing,' he answered dismissively.

When he would have touched his lips to hers, Caroline put her fingers haltingly across his mouth. 'Tell me. I know it's not nothing,' she said astutely.

Sighing, and unable to conceal his frustration, Jack

felt his own expression harden a little as he scanned her anxious, expressive eyes. To admit his heart attack to *Caroline,* of all people, would be tantamount to admitting that he wasn't the great success he'd gone out of his way to prove himself to be. Having always striven to keep himself in A1 physical condition, he would expose the kind of vulnerability that he deliberately guarded against, and it would drag him right back to being the boy her father had so despised from the wrong side of the tracks who in other people's eyes, was 'destined to fail'.

'Do you mind if we *don't* discuss my physical defects right now?' he replied somewhat bitterly, and he watched surprise and hurt infiltrate her lovely face.

'A scar isn't a defect,' Caroline protested softly, her fingers curling into her palm to stop herself from reaching out and gently inspecting the so-called 'defect' that clearly engendered such strong emotion in him. Of course she wanted to know how he had acquired it—was frightened at the idea that it had been caused by something serious—but right now all she could do…all she *longed* to do…was bring him comfort in whatever way she could.

Underneath the outward show of undoubted success, elements of the angry young man Caroline had met and fallen in love with still existed, and it still clearly haunted him. *She sensed it deep down in her very bones.*

'Besides…you look amazing,' she breathed softly, venturing a smile up into that suddenly sombre face of his.

'Are you telling me that you like what you see, sweetheart?'

A smile broke free from his lips that was like a precious glimpse of the sun glimmering through a dark raincloud and, as he ran his palm up the side of her bare leg until it reached the curve of her hip and bottom, she felt his electrifying touch induce a stunning shower of hot little shivers inside her that made her urgently reach towards him, to bring his head down to hers.

Their mouths clashed heatedly, greedily tasting each other as if the world was running out of time, and all thoughts were suspended while pure, uninhibited sensation assumed powerful command.

Pulling down the front of Caroline's nightgown with sudden impatience, Jack fastened his mouth to one tight velvet nipple, then the other, finally surrendering to the insistent demanding need to touch her in the way he had long dreamed of—that tonight had caused him to put his foot down on the accelerator as if his life depended on it all the way back from London, just to be with her.

As his tongue swirled over and hotly dampened the softly quivering flesh, a thunderclap of heat exploded straight into his groin and his swiftly unashamed arousal caused him to emit a hoarse and ragged groan. Exploring her body beneath her thin gown, Jack impatiently pushed the material out of the way before purposefully directing his hand between her thighs, and gently but firmly coaxing them apart.

Her eyes closed of their own volition, to experience

the full devastating wave of erotic pleasure that washed over her as Jack's fingers entered her body—unashamedly stoking the searingly provocative damp heat that flooded into her centre. Caroline silently rejoiced that her most secret heartfelt wish to know the magic of his touch again had come true. But her body tensed as he pressed deeper, her hand instantly grabbing onto his to still it, her heart pumping hard against her ribcage at the realisation that she was still maybe a little too tight for his erection to follow.

Jack wouldn't know that no other man had ever been invited to enjoy the intimacy of touching her as he was doing now, since he had left her seventeen years ago. Her most feminine muscles were not used to being aroused the way he was arousing them at this moment. *And then there was Caroline's deep abiding fear that the termination she had had could have somehow damaged her in some way—even though she'd been given the all-clear by her doctors.*

She didn't doubt that the tremendous guilt she had suffered over the years had played its part in fuelling this fear. It was one reason why she had never allowed herself to get really close to a man in all this time. Besides…there was only *one* man she had ever loved. And even though Jack was here now, doing all the things she yearned for him to do…he didn't love *her.*

'What's the matter?' His deep voice thick with arousal, Jack withdrew his hand and softly touched her face. 'Nothing's wrong, is it?'

Feeling like a terrible fool, Caroline stared up at him, her soft brown eyes unable to contain their fear.

'It's…it's just that it's been such a long time since—' She broke off, feeling her cheeks burn with heat and her throat tighten.

'I *know* how long it's been, Caroline…*seventeen* years.'

Jack's searing glance didn't leave her face for even a moment. But just when Caroline was about to express her relief that he understood, he went on…

'But I'm sure you must have had plenty of practice in between, sweetheart.'

Unable to keep the inevitable derision from his tone, Jack felt half crazy that their lovemaking had been temporarily thwarted, as well as furious that he had been inadvertently forced into thinking about the inevitable fact that Caroline had known other lovers since they had parted. *Why shouldn't she?* She was a stunningly attractive *single* woman. Now, as he regarded her with undeniable frustration, he saw her throat convulse with obvious distress, but he hardened his heart against the sight.

'You—you think I've had other lovers? I know this might be hard for you to believe, Jack…but the truth is I haven't been this intimate with another man since you left.'

The heat from the fire gathered noticeable force and ejected a glowing burning coal that sizzled on the tiled surround.

The impact of her words finally computing in his stunned brain, Jack's gaze narrowed with disbelief.

'You're trying to tell me that I'm the only man you've ever had sex with?'

Hurting abominably that he'd referred to their intimacies so crudely as 'having sex', and not 'making love', Caroline despondently pushed her nightgown back down over her hips and sat up. Threading her trembling fingers through the tumbled golden strands of her long blonde hair, she adjusted the straps of her gown back onto her shoulders and looked suddenly pale.

'Yes, Jack…that's what I'm telling you.'

'I don't believe it.'

'I have no reason to lie.' She shrugged, and her mouth quivered a little.

'If you *are* telling me the truth, Caroline, I want to know why? Why haven't you been with anybody else since we broke up?'

Staring at her as if she was someone he'd never seen before, Jack furrowed his handsome brow.

'I've had boyfriends…of course I have. But I just haven't wanted to sleep with any of them. Is that a crime?'

Feeling chilled to her very bones at the way their passionate reunion was turning out, Caroline stared down at her hands as if they belonged to a stranger. Resting in her lap, they looked too pale…too *unloved,* somehow. If only she had been able to relax a bit more, she anguished miserably. *If only she hadn't worried so much that she wouldn't be able to love him as she yearned to because of her fear…*

But what was the use in condemning herself for her

feelings? She wasn't deliberately trying to be obstructive. She wanted Jack's loving more than she wanted to see daylight after enduring a nightmare alone in the dark! But she was also beginning to think that their brief reunion was utterly doomed.

Looking as if he didn't know whether to believe her or not, Jack sighed heavily.

'And just now…when you stopped me? It was because you were—'

'Like you said, Jack.' Caroline's eyes and her voice were similarly flat. 'Seventeen years is a long time. Can you wonder that I was a little *tense*?'

Before he could say anything, tears were spilling down her cheeks in a steady, agonising flow.

CHAPTER NINE

HE WAS the only man she'd ever properly made love with? Faced with such a momentous revelation, Jack found himself examining Caroline's crestfallen face with an increasing sense of shock. As the pinnacle of that shock ebbed away, he was unable to resist the sudden great need to hold her. Taking her into his arms, Jack cradled her head protectively against his chest.

The last time he'd seen Caroline break her heart in front of him was when she had confessed to having the termination. and he had been so outraged and so destroyed by the news that he had been *stone* to her tears. Now, as well as needing to make love to her more than ever, Jack found her distress the one chink in his armour that he hadn't expected. Emotions were coming to the fore inside him that he'd sworn to keep under lock and key for *good*, and the realisation disturbed him deeply.

'Shh…don't cry…please don't cry.'

Kissing her gently dishevelled blonde head, Jack became a willing slave to the exquisite sensuality of her subtle yet pervasive scent. It was nothing to do with the shampoo or perfume or bath oil she used. It was *everything* to do with Caroline herself. Jack was *undone* by her, and he knew it.

What if he had been too *hasty* in relinquishing her to her fate all those years ago? Coming out of nowhere, it was a stunning, disconcerting thought, and one he wouldn't be at all wise to pursue. Instead, Jack moved Caroline a little way away from him, so that he could glean for himself how she was feeling. Holding onto her arms, he started to seductively massage her skin.

'Explain to me,' he instructed quietly, 'why there hasn't been anyone else?'

Not liking the growing sense of vulnerability that was descending upon her, Caroline realised then that Jack had not been aware of the sheer magnitude and scope of her love for him. Hadn't she shown him enough? Hadn't she *proved* it by giving him her virginity when she was just seventeen? *Maybe he'd thought what she felt for him was just infatuation*? What if that was why he had been able to believe that she had relented 'too easily' to an abortion? If he'd realised how much she had loved him, with all her heart, Jack would have known it could have been nothing less than *torture* to make the decision about their baby. The guilt she'd suffered over that whole distressing episode had tainted almost everything. *Especially* the possibility of ever enjoying an intimate relationship with someone new, or trusting that she wouldn't ever be pressured into terminating a pregnancy again…

'I just—' With the heels of her hands Caroline harshly dismissed the evidence of her tears, suddenly furious that Jack was putting her in such an untenable position. She didn't want to reveal her deepest secrets to him any more. He probably wouldn't believe her anyway, so what was the point? His mind was already made up about her and *nothing* was going to change it. 'Meeting someone and falling in love isn't automatic, you know. I suppose it simply wasn't on the cards…'

Jack didn't know what to think about that. The truth—if he was honest—was that he didn't *want* to speculate too hard about why Caroline had resisted intimacy with other men. Somewhere not too deep inside him he had to admit he was *glad* that she had… and doubly glad that she hadn't fallen in love again…no matter how selfish that might sound. Yet here she was, living in this large old house all by herself, supposedly content with a single life and seeing no one but a man who was old enough to be her father. Jack didn't care how strenuously he denied it—Caroline's doctor friend's interest in her was definitely *not* platonic.

Feeling another jealous wave settle over him, he moved his hands up Caroline's graceful and slender arms to her shoulders and slowly—with a deeply possessive glint in his eye—pulled her flimsy straps back down again. Her soft flesh quivered delightfully, sending another spear of scalding need straight to his groin. He heard her emit a soft, startled breath, and before she could utter a word Jack was kissing her with a stark, ravishing hunger that must have been simmering inside him for *years*.

When he reluctantly slowed things down, to obviously search for protection in his discarded clothing, Caroline's heightened senses descended briefly back down to earth again. *What if they didn't use protection?* If they could make another baby together… If Caroline could only get pregnant again… She would be able to show Jack that her most heartfelt wish was to be the mother of his baby. *A wish she had been cruelly robbed of at her father's shameful and brutal instigation.*

Distressed at the impossible and dangerous direction her thoughts were taking her, Caroline let her gaze cling heatedly to Jack's as with breathtaking expertise he stripped her of her nightgown. Naked in front of him, there was nowhere to hide, and she shivered almost violently as the heat in his eyes licked over her with barely contained lust.

Taking her cue from him, Caroline dipped her gaze to examine the fine display of tight, trained muscle that was so evident in his lean but awesome physique, her stomach jolting in reaction when she saw how aroused he was. Raising her glance level with his again, Caroline was even less able to stop from violently trembling.

'God must have created you just to drive me out of my mind,' he ground out, his voice hoarse with longing. 'But you're in my blood and I can't get you out.'

With a just barely civilised groan, Jack pushed her down onto the rug. In even less time than it had taken to accomplish that, he had settled her beneath him, turning the attention of his expert kisses to her breasts, her ribcage, her sexy tucked-in navel and her hips— skimming over her bones and skin, his mouth and tongue doing things to her body that made Caroline clutch at the rug beneath her to try and stay on the planet.

When he slid his hand between her trembling thighs to part them, his fingers sliding in and out of her wetness with destroying ease, Caroline shut her eyes and no longer *cared* about staying earth-bound. She almost leapt out of her skin when Jack replaced his fingers with his mouth, and nothing could have prepared her for the sheer dazzling violence of the climax his erotic torment finally and inevitably elicited.

All the tension and doubt about whether everything would be okay vanished in a blaze of sensation so strong that Caroline didn't have a prayer when it came to keeping her feelings silent. Crying out with pleasure, she blinked dazedly up at Jack as his firm, muscular thighs straddled her hips. Then he laid passionate siege to her mouth once more.

Her already reeling senses stayed in the ascendant somewhere, circling the heavens. But even as she registered their languid descent Jack had sheathed himself and thrust into her with destroying deliberation. Inevitably Caroline tensed a little at his masculine invasion— for a moment her fears that it might hurt returning—but Jack cleverly seduced her into relaxing, melting any resistance away with amazingly addictive and sublime kisses that left her whimpering for more. Contracting her hot silky muscles around his hard satin length, she felt any trace of lingering anxiety vanish, quickly turning to feelings of pleasure and relief instead. Caroline prayed that Jack now knew with indisputable certainty that he was still her first and only lover.

As he loved her with an intensity that snatched her breath from her lungs—reuniting their bodies even more passionately, it seemed, than he had done all those years ago, when they were both so young— Caroline had to keep reminding herself that she wasn't going to wake up from a dream any time soon—that this blood-stirring erotic encounter was really part of her present and *not* her past.

Sometimes her powerful longing to see Jack again had been so all-consuming that she'd almost believed she could *will* him to come back to her. Now, Caroline wouldn't swear that she'd been able to accomplish any such feat, but even so…she would not discount the possibility of magic. Taking unimaginable delight in simply touching him—in reacquainting her love-starved hands with his powerfully strong body once more—she told herself that even if it all went horribly wrong again she *couldn't* regret this uninhibited loving. In seventeen years she hadn't met *one* other man who had come anywhere *near* making her feel like Jack did.

Knowing that her adoration must be beaming from her gaze like a beacon, Caroline wondered how she was supposed to contain it under these most intimate of circumstances. Whether Jack knew or cared about her feelings or not, she was not adept enough to completely hide them from him. Anchoring her hands around his tautly flexed biceps as he thrust deeply inside her, Caroline watched the passion and purpose intensify on her lover's indisputably charismatic face—every masterfully etched muscle straining to delay the gratification of his desire until her own peak had sent her spinning off into the heavens once more.

Jack was suggesting with gravel-voiced ease that she wrap her long legs around his back—to 'better enjoy the ride, beautiful'—and Caroline didn't hesitate to comply, gasping out loud as desire rose to a whole new level…loving the way the strength in him was brought home to her as she gripped him hungrily with her thighs. Driving himself even deeper, Jack smiled wickedly down at her, giving Caroline no quarter whatsoever. When want, need, and bone-deep desperation to reach the stars found its ultimate reward she cried out again, with every atom of love and longing in her soul, tears slipping helplessly down her face as Jack looked down at her…revealing for just the tiniest moment something like regret or sorrow in his eyes.

Then he bent his head and commandeered Caroline's lips harshly with his own as he ardently surrendered to the need that had been multiplying inside him with ever-increasing command—emptying himself inside her with an echoing shout that wouldn't be contained.

Clearly overcome by the raw, unfettered emotion of

the moment, he laid his head on Caroline's breast and groaned again—his dark silky hair tickling her chin and his strong heartbeat matching hers beat for rhythmic beat. Fear as well as joy swirled inside her chest, and although part of her felt buoyed-up by happiness—at the same time Caroline experienced pain that was like a thousand razor-cuts bleeding into her very soul.

'You always were intoxicating,' Jack whispered husky-voiced against her breast, his warm breath skimming her sensitised skin, 'but you've become even more so.'

'Have I?'

The brief tormented smile that he hadn't witnessed melted away. Staring up in silence at the shadows from the fire, moving like dancing silhouettes on the ceiling, Caroline felt the tears she had cried dry on her cheeks. She would be very 'adult' about what happened, she decided resignedly. She wouldn't make demands or sound 'needy', as he might already be anticipating she would. Fear settled more profoundly in her bones, like a brooding storm deep in her vitals. *He wouldn't stay. She knew that.* So how *did* a person go about forgetting the love of their life, not once but *twice* in a lifetime, without losing their mind?

She'd fallen asleep in his embrace, right there on the rug in front of the fire, giving Jack ample opportunity to study her peaceful sleeping features and to conclude once again that she was *still* the most beautiful girl he'd ever seen. He tried to recall how enraged he had been when she had confessed to having the termination, but right then—sated with the passion they had expended with such uninhibited fervour—Jack found that his anger had somehow diminished.

He didn't doubt that his long-held rage towards Caroline for making the decision that had shaped the course of his life for ever would no doubt resurrect itself once he was away from her sphere of intoxicating influence. In the cold light of day he would remember in detail how she had betrayed him, how she had committed the most unforgivable of actions. But right now…for the first time in a long time…a *lifetime* perhaps?…Jack peacefully surrendered his embittered defences.

For a while he lay there alone with his thoughts, listening to the flurry of wind and rain slam against the windowpanes and inside the soporific 'womb-like' hiss and crackle of the fire burning comfortingly beside them. Then, getting to his feet and being careful not to disturb the woman he'd lain beside, he recovered her fleecy dressing-gown and draped it gently across her sleeping form, so that she wouldn't get cold when the fire went out.

Lord knew it was so *tempting* for Jack to stay right where he was and spend the night there in Caroline's house…the house he had been *barred* from as a youth. If he'd still been immersed in his usual fury towards her and her dead father he would have taken a perverse kind of pleasure in staying there, only to disdainfully leave in the morning. But just what was Jack supposed to say to Caroline when she woke? His store of words was worryingly *empty.* He was, instead, swamped with all kinds of feelings that were taking him by storm. Feelings that he hadn't expected. In the light of this confusion, any words he *did* utter would be like the sound of scraping fingernails down a blackboard. They would be harsh and unpalatable, because his familiar, automatically employed barriers were already slamming into place and Jack knew he would defend his position to the hilt.

Concluding that all he could do was leave Caroline to sleep on undisturbed, he quickly gathered his strewn clothes together, dressed with regretful ease as he watched the soft rise and fall of her breath and glimpsed the smooth alabaster perfection of her breasts beneath her robe, then left the house with the stealth of a thief in the night, to return to his hotel…

Caroline had *known* she was alone, that Jack had left, as soon as she'd opened her eyes. The heat from the fire had noticeably died to barely warm embers that threw off scant comfort, and even though she found herself covered by her dressing-gown she shivered hard as she quickly pushed her arms into its fleecy sleeves and got shakily to her feet. Inside, a silent keening rose up from the emptiness of her heart. Desolation and confusion hit hard. She felt like the only child in a wintry playground being pelted by a bombardment of icy snowballs from her uncaring classmates.

Jack had left her even sooner than she'd thought he would. He hadn't even had the decency to wait until the morning to demonstrate his contempt. Caroline could hardly believe that even *he* could be so heartless. She hadn't been foolish enough to imagine that they might be going to take up where they had left off seventeen years ago, but even so... Jack had seduced her into loving him again one more time, allowed her to let down her defences long enough to fall asleep in his arms, and then—cool as you like—left her there to wake up alone.

Was this particularly cruel behaviour something he had devised on the day that he'd bumped into her? Was it his abominable way of getting back at Caroline for the deep grudge he obviously still bore her? She must have been out of her mind to let him into her house like that in the middle of the night. Now she only had herself to blame for the fall-out. It had been obvious from the start that Jack's reappearance would bring her nothing but more trouble and heartache, but Caroline hadn't been able to resist the compulsion to get burnt by him again. She should have just told him to get the hell out of her life and stay out! Not invite him to make things worse! Why had she done that? *Why?*

'Because I'm a sad, stupid idiot—that's why!' she shouted out loud, kicking the rug. 'He only wanted to get back at me...to hurt me all over again because of what I did...what I was practically *forced* to do! Jack Fitzgerald doesn't possess a forgiving bone in his entire body!'

Giving vent to her frustration and fury, and at the same time making an Olympian effort to suppress the anguished sob that arose inside her throat, Caroline briefly stooped to pick up her crumpled nightdress, then resignedly left the room to go upstairs to bed...

Out of the chaos of scaffolding, cement and mud, the improvements that Jack had devised with his architect for the undeniably neglected Victorian house were slowly but surely taking place. Having just inspected the downstairs area, where a major extension was being built onto the back of the building to utilise some of the space of the three-hundred-foot garden, Jack allowed himself a momentary burst of pleasure and anticipation.

For the last week, being actively involved on site—overseeing building work and having long, productive discussions with the architect and the contractor he'd hired to undertake the renovations—Jack had welcomed long, busy days that started at around seven in the morning and continued long into the evening, when spotlights were rigged up all over the site to replace the fading winter daylight. It had helped him to push the thought of Caroline and what he was going to do about the confusion of feelings he felt towards her out of his mind at least temporarily.

One thing was crystal-clear. She must think him a contemptuous bastard for leaving before she woke the other night, and not even saying goodbye. But, as he'd silently admitted to himself at the time, he wouldn't have known what to say to her after what had transpired between them…what should *never* have transpired between them if it hadn't been for the fact that Jack had allowed his *lust* for her to tow him round by the nose…

He'd needed time to assimilate everything that had happened. By now, she must *hate* his guts…

Stepping out of the luxurious hotel room shower and winding a generous white bathtowel around his spare, taut midsection, Jack paused to examine his sombre reflection as he passed the large bathroom mirror. To say he didn't like what he saw would be massive understatement.

When he looked into his own glacial blue eyes in the harshly delineated planes and angles of his sculpted, lean face, Jack despised the fear and control he saw reflected there. *Fear* that had been generated by driving his body almost into the ground, with his ruthless ambition to rise above his poor beginnings, and that had shockingly culminated in a heart attack. A 'warning shot', if you like, that had told him he had to either lessen that suicidal drive of his to a more reasonable degree or pay the consequences. And a rigid *control* that meant he hardly ever allowed himself to experience tender or loving feelings towards anybody. A control that had dictated he walk away from the one woman who *did* stir strong feelings inside him because he still believed she couldn't be trusted.

Giving vent to a ripe expletive as he reached for the can of shaving foam on the marble ledge beside the mirror, Jack glanced up and frowned as he heard a knock at the door. Crossing the thickly carpeted bedroom in his bare feet, and walking out into the luxurious sitting room that made up his suite of rooms, Jack pulled open the door with hardly any curiosity at all. He'd ordered coffee and brandy to be brought up to his suite in about half an hour but obviously his order had arrived a little early. However, the way he was feeling, Jack could do with a strong drink *sooner* rather than later, to help dull the pain of unwanted thoughts that were right now driving him crazy. He wasn't supposed to drink, given what had happened to him, but *hell*... he'd never been attracted to alcohol the way some of his equally driven business associates were. A little brandy wouldn't hurt.

'Caroline!'

He was honestly stunned to see her there.

'Hello, Jack...this is for the other night.'

Before he could glean what she meant, Caroline had raised her hand and delivered a stinging, resounding slap hard across his face...

CHAPTER TEN

SHE HADN'T gone to Jack's hotel with the express intention of slapping his face. But the minute that Caroline had been confronted by his disturbing presence, and the expression that was far too relaxed for her liking crossing his handsome features, she'd realised how powerfully close her emotions were to the surface.

She'd soared to the highest of heights in the past week, just thinking about their lovemaking, and sunk to the lowest of lows as well, when she'd continued not to hear from him. Finally, unable to wait a minute longer to set the record straight once and for all, and tell Jack exactly what she thought of him, Caroline had decided she wasn't going to waste another *second*…let alone another *day* on thoughts of the callous, unforgiving man who was causing her such grief. The man who had walked out on her when she was at her most scared and vulnerable seventeen years ago and had then exhibited the same despicable behaviour again just days ago! And what was more…Caroline was going to spare him nothing when she told him so to his face!

Rubbing his stinging jaw with a wry smirk, Jack stepped back from the door.

'I guess you could say that I deserved that. Well… why don't you come on in, Caroline? My guess is that you have a lot more that you want to say to me than that… Am I right?'

'No.' The blood rushed to her head with such emotive force that Caroline's balance was momentarily at risk. 'You're wrong. I've suddenly decided that I'm not going to waste another word or even another *breath* on you, Jack! Because you know what? You're not *worth* it!'

About to turn around and leave, she was shocked by the powerful grip that Jack used on her wrist, to practically haul her into the room. 'What do you think you're—?'

'You're not going anywhere until we've talked.'

The door slammed shut. His hard jaw like immovable granite, he glared at her, openly daring her to defy him.

Shaking off his hold on her wrist, Caroline pushed her hair behind her ears and scowled. 'Bit late in the day for talking, isn't it, Jack?' she remarked scathingly. 'As I recall…it's not exactly your forte, is it? Either talking about feelings *or* doing the decent thing!'

Wishing that she had found him a little more *clothed* than he was currently so that they would be more on an equal footing, as it were, Caroline felt her legs treacherously shaking as he trained his cynical glance upon her hot, indignant face.

'And who are *you* to talk about doing the "decent thing", Caroline?'

As soon as the words were out of his mouth, Jack wished that his seemingly innate ability to wound her was not quite so lethally accurate. The colour seemed to seep away from her face before his very eyes, and she actually swayed a little. Her hand moved shakily down over her hip, and Jack's gaze was helplessly ensnared by the way the black velvet material of her trouser suit so sexily encased her gorgeous figure. The brightness of her hair glowed like living sunshine, and was an arresting contrast to the dramatic severity of the black. Even in the middle of the most excruciating tension between them he couldn't help but be aroused by her beauty.

'You are such a bastard.'

Her words…so softly yet devastatingly spoken… were like hammer-blows to Jack's soul. To counteract his escalating misery, he deliberately let loose a slow but savage smile.

'What? You think you're the first person to label me with that tag? So sorry to have to disappoint you.'

'And you're proud of that?' Caroline swallowed across the stinging pain inside her throat as though it were a landscape filled with cacti. 'I feel sorry for you… always having to appear so hard, so tough. You may have achieved everything you've ever wanted, but I'd stake my house on it that it hasn't made you happy. Bitterness can eat you up, you know. You have a cold, unforgiving heart, Jack, and the way I see it now...I've probably had a lucky escape, haven't I?'

Hands on his hips, Jack briefly glanced down at the carpet, as if trying to restrain the temper she seemed hell-bent on rousing. When he regarded Caroline again, the steely blue eyes that couldn't help but command attention reminded her of a hard frost that hadn't thawed all winter, and her blood actually ran cold.

'Why didn't you come and tell me you'd decided on having a termination, Caroline? Why didn't you talk it over with me instead of just going ahead and doing it? I was the baby's father...didn't you think I should have any say in the matter at all?'

For a long, distraught moment everything inside Caroline seemed to shudder violently. Staring at him with undeniable agony in her dark gaze, she was forced to remember the distressing and frightening circumstances that had led her to check in to that soulless, aloof private hospital in London, where they had removed the growing foetus inside her as coldly and dispassionately as if she'd been having a mole or adhesion taken away.

'Of *course* I believed you had the right to have a say! And, contrary to what you might think, I *wanted* to keep the baby...that's why I told my father that I was pregnant. If there had been a way to keep it don't you think I would have? But he—he just went crazy when I told him.'

She smiled nervously, to try and calm her quivering

lips, but the smile slid off her face as easily as a raindrop sliding down a windowpane. Checking behind her, Caroline saw a Queen-Anne-style armchair covered in a pattern of cream and pink rosebuds and gratefully sank down into it. Her legs were shaking so hard that she felt as if she'd been ploughed into by a rhinoceros. Knowing that she had Jack's full undivided attention, as she'd never had it before, she took a painful swallow and tried desperately to pluck out a coherent strand of thought from the black cloud of hurtful memory that was pressing in on her with such unforgiving force.

'People thought he was marvelous, you know…how kind, how *understanding*. Well…he *was* like that with his patients and his friends…but *not* me. My mother died giving birth to me…did I ever tell you that?' Her dark eyes glistening, Caroline looked straight at Jack.

'No.' He folded his arms across his chest—the movement drawing her attention to the tight, mouth-watering curve of his biceps—and his dispassionate expression contained neither warmth or understanding.

Ignoring his blatant lack of encouragement or support, Caroline pressed determinedly on. 'I think he blamed me because he lost her. In fact I *know* he did. It was no secret. She was so beautiful, and they were so in love. Then *I* came along and put an end to their happiness together… Anyway, when I told Dad that I was pregnant he completely lost his reason. Actually…' She grimaced and linked her hands nervously together in her lap. 'That's a bit of an understatement, if you want to know the truth. His anger just escalated into something—something quite *ugly*. He hit me hard, and knocked me to the ground.'

'He *what*?'

'He *made* me have the abortion, Jack. He couldn't stand the shame of it, he said.'

Jack's stomach plummeted violently, as though he'd just been pushed off the top of a skyscraper. *This wasn't happening…she wasn't saying what she was saying…it couldn't be real…* He didn't doubt that her father had gone crazy when he'd heard that his seventeen-year-old daughter was pregnant…and by a boy whose very existence he *despised*…but if Jack had thought for one second that the man—a *doctor*, for God's sake!—would coerce his own flesh and blood into having an abortion, then he wouldn't have been so quick to judge the woman he loved and punish her even further by walking away for good. Now Jack realised that they should have faced her father together. It was *unthinkable* that he'd let her confront him alone.

'Maybe he hoped that the shock of his attack might make me lose the baby…or—or maybe he didn't think at all. He was simply too furious with me. I'd shamed him, he said. I'd let him down and made him look like a fool. He said didn't I *know* that boys like you didn't stick around after they'd had their fun? I was no better than a—than a whore and a slut and I'd throw away every chance of a decent marriage if I didn't get rid of the baby. He told me I had no choice but to do what he said. He left me alone then, and went to make a phone call. The next morning he drove me to London and it was done.'

When her haltingly voiced explanation was over, Caroline leaned back in the chair—the beautiful and elegant piece of furniture that lent such a contrasting civility to her painfully sordid revelation—and briefly shut her eyes. There were no words to describe either the psychological pain of having her own father assault her *or* the physical hurt that she'd endured—both from the attack and afterwards the abortion. Now, having told Jack the truth behind her actions all those years ago, Caroline was emotionally and physically drained of everything. She just prayed he wouldn't be expecting her to get up and go anywhere for the next ten minutes at least, because it was doubtful whether her legs would have the strength required to enable her to stand, let alone walk.

'Sweet heaven, Caroline! Why didn't you tell me all this before?'

His senses reeling in protest at what he had just heard, Jack made his feet stay rooted to the floor as he watched her wearily close her eyes again—as if she didn't know what else to do after such a revelation. Everything that was decent and good inside him clamoured for him to go to her…haul her into his arms, keep her safe and never let her go. But now that he realised for the first time in seventeen years that it was *he* who had betrayed Caroline—by not staying around to find out the truth before packing his bags and heading off to

a completely different continent never to look back—
Jack couldn't do it.

He'd condemned her. He'd relinquished all right to
comfort her when he'd walked out on her to ruthlessly
pursue his dream of wealth and status—to fight his own
demons of poverty and shame and command respect
from the world instead of disdain. Well, he'd achieved
his ambition in spades, and it still hadn't filled the
yawning chasm inside him that craved something much
less tangible yet *infinitely* more valuable. Something
that he'd allowed his single-minded ambition to over-
ride…*no doubt to his detriment.* Caroline's house was
safe. She could easily stake it on her bet that his wealth
hadn't made him happy and she'd be absolutely right.

Jack remembered the night she had come to him and
told him that she'd had the abortion. He hadn't seen her
for two days—her father had slammed the door in his
face when he'd gone to their house to ask after her
whereabouts, and Jack had been beside himself with
worry. His stomach muscles gripped with a vengeance
as he suddenly recalled the pain and sorrow in her beautiful dark eyes when he'd finally seen her…but more
than that…the vivid purple bruise on the side of her
delicate jaw. Caroline had told him that it was nothing,
that she'd accidentally walked into a door when she'd
been hurrying and not looking where she was going. For
that read…*running away from her father to avoid
further mistreatment*?

The thought was akin to a nuclear meltdown inside

Jack. Automatically, his hands clenched into fists at his side. *That cruel bastard.* If he was here now Jack would willingly do time in prison for what he would do to him in recompense…

Opening her eyes, Caroline pushed her fingers through her hair and softly sighed.

'You weren't ready to listen,' she told him in answer to his impassioned question. 'You were always so sure you were right about everything, and you were so hungry to get away from here and make your mark on the world. I told myself after you'd left that it was probably for the best. Me having a baby would only have made you feel obliged to stay, and I know you'd never wanted that. But you know what, Jack? Just for the record…my father didn't just look down on *you.* Until a few years before his death I was a great disappointment to him too. I wouldn't let him mould me like he wanted to. I wouldn't aspire to the things he thought I should aspire to. But we reached a kind of unspoken accord after a while, and he didn't try to interfere in my life any more. He left me the house and some money in his will—to try and make amends, I'm sure.'

'It's a wonder you can even bear to live in it!' Jack remarked with bitterness, a wealth of regret and a soul-deep sorrow crowding his chest so strongly that he barely knew how to ease it. All he could think was that he'd possibly made the worst decision of his life when he'd walked out so callously on Caroline. He believed her father to have been a cruel bastard, but perhaps the truth in Jack's case was that it *took* one to know one?

'I told myself that if my mother had lived *she* would have wanted me to have the house too. Anyway…every child loves their parents, don't they? All a child really wants is their love and approval, and they'll forgive even violence against them to get it. I forgave my father everything the day he died. He acted like he did because he was hurting…because he'd lost my mother. Only hurt people hit out at others.'

'Your compassion is a credit to you, Caroline…but I'll tell you for the life of me I can't understand it.'

'Well…'

Feeling as if he'd judged her again, and found her completely lacking in any universally accepted common sense, Caroline forced herself to think about leaving. She couldn't sit here in this chair for ever, and she couldn't make the wrong between her and Jack right again just because her heart ached to do just that. Now she really had to show her quality, and demonstrate just how strong she really was. Strong enough to make her life a success without him. Strong enough to put what they had once so joyfully shared down to experience and move on. Undoubtedly she was a talented, capable woman, and she would show the world that no matter what happened—no one else would ever knock her down, or *put* her down again.

'We all have our own ways of looking at things, don't we? Even though it might seem skewed to others. I won't keep you any longer. I'd best just get going.'

'No…wait!'

Panic made Jack's blue eyes glitter and his hard jaw tighten even more. She couldn't just walk in here, deliver such a gut-wrenching bombshell and then go. He wouldn't *let* her. He'd been a fool, an idiot, selfish and self-seeking even… But what Caroline had revealed to him had rocked his world harder than an earthquake.

'Why, Jack? What for?' She pushed to her feet, her pale cheeks reddening a little. 'Five days ago you knocked at my house in the middle of the night, asked me not to turn you out into the cold, made love to me…then left while I was asleep. I woke up to a dying fire and an empty space beside me. There was no hint *why*. When I examined all the possible reasons, I concluded that you were getting your own back on me, and no doubt you *were*. You amply illustrated that I wasn't even deserving of the most *basic* respect. I only came here to tell you that I *refuse* to be blamed for what happened any longer. And I refuse to spend the rest of my days carrying the burden of that blame and letting it spoil my life! I have plans, Jack…plans that might take me only God knows where…and now I just want to go home and get on with them. I'll see myself out.'

As she reached the door Jack stared at her stiff back and tried desperately to command the words that were rapidly backing up in his brain, practically tripping over each other. He knew what he *should* say…what he *longed* to be able to say… But he already sensed her moving away from him in more ways than one, and he wouldn't expose his needs to possible derision…even though he no doubt richly *deserved* it.

'What do you mean, you've got "plans"?' he demanded, his frustration peppering the words with anger. 'Do they include that doctor friend of yours? The one who's old enough to be your father?'

Slowly Caroline turned around, for once her expression unreadable. 'You mean Nicholas?' She sighed.

Even the man's name had the power to practically unhinge Jack. He'd seen the way he'd looked at Caroline that night when they'd been having dinner together at his hotel. The man's glance had been nothing less than *predatory*... 'platonic', indeed!

'I believe that is his name.'

'I honestly don't think it's any of your business...do you?'

Caroline opened the door and went out, shutting it behind her.

Cursing the fact that he wasn't dressed—hardly fit to chase after her when he was wearing nothing but a towel—Jack forced his fevered brain to work overtime and think what to do next...

The winter sun, shining powerfully through the back window of Caroline's store room, illuminated the vivid display of colour that she'd been painting onto a canvas. Taking a moment to consider her handiwork, she allowed herself a triumphant pleased smile. She'd been finding out a lot about butterflies in the past couple of days, and the more she discovered about their symbolism and meaning—as well as their biological make-up—the more intrigued Caroline had become by them.

It was the symbolism of *transformation* that had captured her interest the most. The caterpillar spun a cocoon in which to birth a new aspect of itself—then, when the time was right...after a time of what some might call spiritual waiting, it emerged into the light and a new beginning as a beautiful butterfly.

Caroline had undertaken the painting as a gift she might give to Sadie. The shy, unconfident schoolgirl was blossoming into a woman...she was on the brink of falling in love, perhaps, and the future seemed bright. For a moment Caroline remembered that feeling of infinite possibilities in the world and felt her breath catch. But a strange thing was happening. Because the more she stroked paint onto the canvas, the more the bright colours inspired her imagination and made her hopes for her *own* future soar...and the more Caroline saw that the painting was also a gift to herself.

She'd already decided that in the spring she would put both the house and the shop up for sale. 'Infinite possibilities' awaited her too, and she would use some of the money she made from the sales of her property to maybe explore some of them. She might even buy herself a round-the-world ticket...who knew?

But what about Jack? The smile on her face faded slowly away as her thoughts turned to the one topic that put a hitch in her excited plans. When she'd left his hotel room yesterday she'd dragged her feet as she'd walked away, hoping…*praying*…that he might say something that would make her stop walking away from him… something that might herald even the *tiniest* ray of hope for them both. *It hadn't happened*, and finally… *finally*…Caroline had had to tell herself that their relationship was irretrievably over. All she could hope was that Jack could go back to wherever he lived now and perhaps think of her with a little more forgiveness in his heart than he had previously extended to his memory of her. She didn't think she could bear it if all his thoughts of her were negative ones.

With her paintbrush hovering over a dazzlingly brilliant blue section of a butterfly, Caroline was taken aback by the jolt of fear that suddenly assaulted her. *That scar on Jack's chest was over his heart…* Why hadn't she realised that before? With a trembling hand she laid the sable-haired brush she was using down on the easel's shelf and walked like someone in a trance out of the store room and back into the shop to find the telephone…

CHAPTER ELEVEN

'SOMEONE to see you, Mr Fitzgerald.'

Frank Ryan, the site foreman, ambled over to Jack where he stood by the side of the house, examining some plans with his architect.

'Who is it?' Barely glancing up from the drawings that were occupying him, Jack frowned at having his train of thought interrupted.

'Didn't ask, guv'nor.' Frank shrugged, as if to indicate it was none of his business. 'He's waiting for you over there.'

He pointed to where the cement mixer chugged, on the paving stones leading up to the house, and Jack did a surprised double-take when he recognised Nicholas Brandon...Caroline's doctor friend. Wearing an expensive-looking double-breasted pin-striped suit, he appeared both uncomfortable and on edge as he paced up and down, looking about as out of place in what was in effect a building site as a diamond brooch pinned to the shirt of a vagrant.

'Give me a couple of minutes will you, Justin?'

Handing over the plans to his architect—Jack made his way past the general melee of rubble and sand to greet his unexpected visitor.

'What can I do for you?'

It was a terse demand rather than a civil greeting. He snapped out the words as though barely able to spare the time to talk, even while his blue eyes weighed and assessed and weighed again. *What did Caroline see in him?* Jack thought resentfully. The man had a weak chin and shifty eyes. The thought of him even fantasising about Caroline—let alone *touching* her—was apt to make Jack feel ready to knock his head from his shoulders.

'I've come to talk to you about Caroline,' Nicholas began, clearly taken aback by Jack's less than polite acknowledgement.

Wrong answer, Jack concluded in silence, his resentment escalating.

'What about Caroline?'

'You should stay away from her. She was perfectly happy until you showed up again.' Fingering the knot of his tie, Nicholas jerked his chin a little, as if to add emphasis to his advice. 'You've caused her enough trouble as it is. Why did you come back here, Fitzgerald? Why didn't you just stay wherever it is the devil took you? You made a bloody nuisance of yourself seventeen years ago when you were here, and caused her and her family untold grief!'

'I have a suggestion for you, Dr Brandon. Why don't you mind your own damn business and stay out of mine?'

Feeling his spine tense, as though a steel rod had been jammed down his back to replace it, Jack knew his ire was well and truly provoked. He took exceeding umbrage at the fact that this man standing before him should even *dare* to raise the subject of Jack's relationship with Caroline and what had happened in the past. His mercurial eyes directed a deliberately menacing glint.

'Caroline *is* my business,' Nicholas insisted. 'She's a good friend, and so was her father.'

'If her father was a good friend of yours then I *pity* you.'

'What do you mean by that? Charles Tremayne was a good, decent man, and I remember what you put him through,' Nicholas responded, with self-righteous indignation.

'Is that right?'

Edging closer, Jack was satisfied that his superior height, breadth of shoulder and comparative youth were enough to intimidate the other man, even if his words didn't help the message filter through. It gave him untold satisfaction to see Nicholas Brandon flinch.

'Well...did your "good, decent" friend happen to tell you about the "untold grief" and hurt he caused his own daughter? No...I didn't think so.'

'What are you talking about?' the other man replied defensively, turning a little red in the face. 'Charles loved Caroline! He would never have deliberately caused her pain. If you're referring to her having the pregnancy terminated…it was for the best. When he told me what he'd decided I totally supported his decision. A pregnancy would have ruined her life at that point, and Charles knew you weren't the sort of chap to stand by his daughter. You already had a bit of a reputation and it wasn't an admirable one, Fitzgerald!'

So this friend of Caroline's…this pompous little weasel…had colluded with her father to make her have the abortion? A red mist was starting to come down over Jack's furious eyes.

'What the hell did you know about me that you thought you had the right to judge me…hmm? You, with your comfortable upper-crust existence, who probably never got your hands dirty or went hungry in your whole life! But that aside…you have the bloody bare-faced audacity to stand in front of me and tell me that you colluded with Caroline's father to make her have that abortion? You *both* had the temerity to make that decision over our heads?'

'Don't try and tell me that you welcomed the idea of becoming a father!' Nicholas's tone was scornful. 'You were probably *grateful* that we'd got you off the hook, so that you could disappear into the wide blue yonder, untroubled by your conscience, leaving Caroline to shoulder all the blame!'

Jack went cold as the grave. His eyes narrowing to burning blue chips of glittering glass, he stared the other man down as though his glance alone could render him dead.

'Do you know how lucky you are to be still standing there in one piece? If it wasn't for the fact that I really don't think you're even worth the trouble, I'd leave you in need of medical services for the rest of your natural life, Brandon. But then I guess if I descended to that I'd be as bad as Caroline's father, wouldn't I? At least my one redeeming quality is that I don't get my kicks out of beating up defenceless women, like he did!'

'Beating up defenceless wom—? What on earth are you talking about?' Nicholas was looking about as nervous as a man could get, and there was genuine alarm in his gaze. 'Charles didn't hit women!'

'The night Caroline went to him to tell him that she was pregnant, he hit her so hard he knocked her to the floor!'

'Who told you such a despicable lie?'

'Caroline told me herself. Do you really think that she would make something like that up? If you know her at all, then you know she doesn't find it easy to lie…except maybe to protect those she loves. She had a bruise the size of a small country on her pretty face when she came to tell me she'd had the abortion. She told me she'd accidentally walked into a door. You know what the truth is, Brandon? We *all* let her down… her father, you, me… We make a fine bunch, don't we?'

The backs of his eyes burning with unshed tears, Jack threw the man a last pitying glance before striding back towards the house.

* * *

She'd agreed to have dinner with Nicholas at a new Mexican restaurant that had recently opened in the high street. She hadn't wanted to make a big deal of her request to see him, but when she'd rung and told him she needed to talk to him he'd insisted that he take her out to dinner, and he had been the one to suggest the venue. Quite honestly Caroline had been totally surprised by his choice. Nicholas was conservative with a capital 'C', and generally didn't express interest in so-called 'foreign' cuisine.

When Caroline had asked him the reason for his preference, he'd said lightly, 'Perhaps I've become a little too set in my ways…maybe I should try new things more often? They do say it helps keep you young.'

It hadn't been hard to detect that he wanted to please her. Glad that he was being warm and friendly, and not bearing any grudge towards her for turning down his request to get engaged, Caroline was relieved that their friendship could continue without any undercurrent of difficulty or resentment. Feeling determined to present a much more positive and upbeat image than of late, to emphasise her newfound determination to recreate her life, she wore a long, tiered ethnic-style skirt in warm browns and reds, with a black velvet top and boots, and finished off the ensemble with a pair of jet earrings shaped like teardrops.

'You look very lovely tonight, if you don't mind my saying so.'

A brief flare of peculiar intensity in his glance,

Nicholas took a long sip of his Margarita—another choice that had surprised Caroline. Generally he always selected wine when they went out to eat, and didn't really touch spirits as a rule—except for an occasional snifter of the good malt he kept in his surgery drawer. She'd certainly never seen him imbibe a cocktail before. Somehow a drink like that seemed far too frivolous for someone like him.

Flushing a little at the unexpected compliment, Caroline surveyed her companion across the dinner table with slight unease, and for the first time realised that he appeared uncharacteristically nervous.

'Thank you.'

A lively salsa tune filled the small, rather intimate restaurant from hidden speakers, and Caroline mused that it was another thing that somehow seemed totally at odds around someone like her companion—a man who was a bit of a self-confessed snob about music, who believed there was no music worth listening to other than classical.

Nicholas considered the beautiful vivacious girl seated opposite him and couldn't help but feel his blood quicken. Over the years, he'd watched her blossom from a pretty, engaging teenager into a stunning and graceful woman. There had been many times when he and Meg had yearned to have a daughter just like Caroline, but sadly they had not been blessed with children of their own. Then, after Meg had died, Nicholas had slowly started to see Caroline in a completely different light.

His feelings of friendship had deepened into something much more meaningful…something that had quite taken him by surprise. He'd always felt protective of her, and when she'd had that sordid little affair with Fitzgerald Nicholas had been as concerned and furious as Charles, and had breathed a deep sigh of relief when he'd heard that the young tearaway had left home for good and that Caroline would likely never see him again.

It had honestly shaken him to discover that Jack Fitzgerald was back and that he was apparently renovating the old run-down house he'd used to live in with his mother. Having seen the project for himself earlier today, Nicholas saw that the man was clearly pouring plenty of money into the rebuild. He'd easily recognised the name of the contractors he was employing from the livery emblazoned on their vans, and they were about the best in the country. Wherever Fitzgerald had been for the past seventeen years, he'd clearly achieved some wealth and status, and the realisation burned like bile in the pit of Nicholas's stomach.

He'd been disappointed…yes…that Caroline had turned down his suggestion of an engagement, but his hopes had not been seriously dashed. She clearly just needed time to get used to the idea, and he wasn't going to let a jumped-up, swaggering upstart like Jack Fitzgerald come between them…no matter how threatening the man appeared. It had been a real boost to his ego to have her call him today and ask to see him, and he wouldn't be human if he didn't have hopes that she might have reconsidered his offer.

'Anyway…as delighted as I am to have your company, my dear, you sounded as if you were quite concerned about something on the phone earlier. What was it you wanted to talk to me about?'

'I—I just need a little medical advice, if you don't mind?'

Caroline immediately saw the flare of hope that she'd earlier recognised in Nicholas's hazel eyes suddenly dim. It was obvious to her that he had thought she wanted to reconsider the offer he'd made, and her stomach helplessly flipped. There was something about the man tonight that put her on edge. But she had to find a way of bypassing her uneasiness, because she was desperate for some information. Ever since she'd seen that scar on Jack's chest she had been worried about the reason behind it. He clearly did not want to divulge that reason himself, and so she was being forced to try and make some sort of educated guess. Hence her need to speak with Nicholas.

'I'm only glad to give you any advice I can, my dear…you know that.'

'Well, then…I wondered if you could tell me something about heart attacks?'

'Heart attacks, Caroline?' Frowning, Nicholas considered her anxious face intently. 'Do you know someone who has suffered one?'

She sighed and tucked some of her tantalising golden

curls behind her ear. 'Please, Nicholas…can you just give me some information?'

'Well…they happen when the heart muscle fails because the blood flow to the heart becomes blocked. There are a number of ways we can treat them…medication to increase blood flow, for instance, or surgery to open the arteries to the heart. If the patient is willing and determined to improve their lifestyle—to stop smoking, cut down on stress and eat a more healthy diet with less saturated fats—then there's no reason why they can't continue to live a normal life. Does that answer your question?'

She told herself she should be feeling relieved. People weren't automatically going to die young if they'd suffered a heart attack early on in life. There were lifestyle changes that could be made—Nicholas had just outlined them. *But how could Caroline feel relieved when clearly Jack's lifestyle up until now must have been impossibly stressful to have caused him to need heart surgery at the too young age of thirty-seven in the first place?* She already knew that he was angry and bitter about what had happened between them. If he'd been carrying around that rage inside him all these years and on top of that the stress of a demanding job, then no wonder he had suffered a heart problem!

Caroline had read in a self-help book she'd bought that one of the possible metaphysical causes of a heart attack was when a heart felt deprived of joy due to a person's pursuit of making money over everything else…that, plus long-standing emotional problems that eventually helped harden the heart. When you added all that up, Jack was a prime candidate for what had happened to him.

What could she do to help? Caroline bit down on her lip, deep in thought. Had he thought about what she'd said to him about forgiveness? Had he really taken on board the fact that she forgave him for blaming her all these years? Had he heard the truth in her voice when she'd related the distressing circumstances behind her seemingly hasty and callous decision to have the abortion, and was he even *halfway* to letting all that bitterness towards her go?

'You seem miles away, my darling.'

Reaching for her hand, Nicholas seemed a little peeved at her lack of attention towards him. Retrieving her hand and subconsciously rubbing it, Caroline smiled a little distractedly. 'I'm sorry, Nicholas…yes, that does answer my question, thank you. You've been very helpful.'

Now Nicholas looked pained. 'That sounds terribly formal, my dear, if you don't mind my saying? I'm delighted to be able to give you any help I can…I'm your *friend*, remember?'

But one day soon I hope to be a lot more than that… He summoned up a smile that he felt would be perfectly reassuring to her, and was slightly taken aback when he saw Caroline frown instead.

'Yes, Nicholas…you *are* my friend…a very dear and important friend. And I would like us to stay that way, if you don't mind?' Keeping her dark gaze steady, she sighed softly. 'I couldn't ever marry you and risk spoiling that special bond we have between us. And besides…I have to tell you that I'm in love with someone else.'

A muscle twitched beneath Nicholas's eye. Caroline could tell he was having some difficulty in keeping his temper in check. Her stomach sank like a stone.

'You mean Fitzgerald, don't you? I can't believe that you'd be so foolish as to pin all your hopes on a happy union with that despicable man! He's already hurt you beyond repair, Caroline…please don't make the same mistake twice!'

Swallowing down her embarrassment and disappointment that her friend should display such vehement emotion towards the idea of her having a relationship with Jack, Caroline resolved to draw a line under the discussion for good.

'I'm sorry you feel so strongly about it, Nicholas, but I know what I'm doing…I know what I want. And it doesn't matter if it should turn out that Jack doesn't want the same thing. I *still* love him.' She flushed pink. 'I'll probably *always* love him, if you want to know the truth. The question is now…do you still want us to be friends, or will my confession make things too awkward on your part for our friendship to continue?'

Examining his menu, her companion looked at it in secret horror. It was not his cup of tea at all! In fact he wished he'd never suggested coming here in the first place. He wished it even more vehemently since things had definitely *not* gone the way he'd privately hoped that they would!

'I would be a liar if I told you I wasn't upset by your admission of love for this man, Caroline… But frankly I'd be completely shooting myself in the foot if I told you I wanted our friendship to come to an end because of it. If I am truly the friend I have always felt myself to be towards you, then all I can really want is your happiness, my dear. So we will leave things at that, shall we? Now I suppose we'd better order some food. What shall we have? I think I might just have to call over the waitress to help us make a choice…'

Jack was pacing…his expensive Italian hand-made shoes all but wearing a chasm in the plush hotel carpet. He wanted to see Caroline, and the need was like a forest fire raging. But when she'd left him yesterday there had been a resolve and determination in her bewitching dark eyes and in her voice that Jack had never witnessed before. *She was clearly hell-bent on making a new life that didn't include him in any way.* When she'd told him she had plans, and then refused to elaborate on what they were, he'd been truly worried that she was going to leave town without telling him. But then, when he'd calmed himself down, he'd thought, *What can she do? She's got a house and a business to take care of…she can't just take off and not tell anyone…can she?*

Continuing to pace, Jack thought about his confrontation earlier in the day with Nicholas Brandon and wanted to throw something. There were plenty of pretty *objets d'art* in his luxurious hotel suite that would double up as missiles, but again Jack remembered his blood pressure. It wouldn't do him any good getting riled up about that pathetic little weasel. He valued his health far too much these days, he realized, to jeopardise it over such an insignificant excuse for a human being as Brandon. Just as long as he kept away from Caroline Jack would be happy.

He let loose a ripe curse at the idea that he might not, then scraped his fingers irritably through dark hair that had already borne the brunt of his impatience. 'Get a grip, Fitzgerald...you know what you have to do.'

For a moment his gut burned at the memory of what Caroline had told him about her father and how he'd treated her that fateful night she'd told him about her pregnancy. *If he could have turned back the clock Jack would have been there for her, protecting her, persuading her to come away with him and start a new life.* Instead Jack had chosen to blame her, instead of supporting her, and then he'd left. *She'd been just seventeen years old, for heaven's sake! A young, innocent girl and everyone around her had let her down...* But Jack had let her down the most.

Impatient to do what he should have done yesterday, when Caroline had walked out of his hotel room—an action he'd hesitated over far too long because of his fears of a destroying and negative outcome—Jack stopped wearing a hole in the carpet, grabbed his leather jacket and headed out of the door into the corridor, and towards the lift.

Driving his car down the high street on his way to Caroline's place, he almost screeched to a halt when he saw her come out of the Mexican restaurant with its newly painted signage swinging from a bracket overhead. She was being followed out by none other than the famous doctor himself, his hand possessively at her back as they started to walk away beneath the illumination of the streetlights.

An indescribable wave of jealousy and rage snatched the breath from Jack's lungs—his immediate instinct was to park the car and chase after them, and give Nicholas Brandon the comeuppance he richly deserved. *What was she doing out with him?* he thought savagely. Caroline was *his*…didn't she know that?

Quashing the urge to follow them as swiftly as the urge had arisen, Jack decided to bide his time instead and follow her home. He didn't allow himself to consider for one moment that she might be going home with the doctor. If that was her intention, then he would simply have to act to prevent it.

Thankfully his instincts turned out to be right. Nicholas dropped Caroline outside her front door, briefly kissed her goodbye on the side of her cheek…*much to Jack's pain*…then got into his car and drove away again.

As she put her key into the lock, Jack left the driver's seat of his own car, slammed the door shut behind him and hurried up the drive.

'Caroline,' he breathed behind her.

'Jack!' Swinging round, her key left in the lock, she knew her dark eyes registered her surprise and confusion. 'What are you doing here?'

'I had to see you.'

'Why?'

'I'm not talking out here. Open the door and let's go inside.'

'But you—'

'Open the damn door, Caroline!'

Turning the key in the lock himself, Jack pushed open the door and dragged Caroline in behind him. Kicking it shut with the heel of his shoe, he let his heated gaze scan her indignant countenance, feeling no small amount of desire scorching through his blood. *God, she was so beautiful!* How could he have walked out on her as he had? Jack hardly *knew* the man who had done that.

'You had to see me about what?'

As she backed up against the wall, a puzzled angry frown appeared between Caroline's smooth dark blonde brows.

'For someone who despises me you seem to be extraordinarily attached to following me around!'

'Never mind that. What were you doing out with that creep Nicholas Brandon?'

They weren't the words that Jack had wanted to say first, but somehow they'd got in the way of his real intent and acted like an incendiary going off in his face.

He saw the splinters from the explosion make her shiver, and clearly registered the hurt and disappointment in her shocked glance.

'You are unbelievable—do you know that? What business is it of yours who I go out to dinner with? My life is my own, and I don't have to answer to you, Jack Fitzgerald!'

'Do you like him?' he demanded. 'Are you in love with him?' He could hardly bear to hear her answer.

Caroline stared at him as if hardly computing the question.

Driven way past any ability to be patient—*and that particular commodity had always been in short supply in his case*—Jack grabbed her by the shoulders and impelled her roughly against his chest. 'Answer me, goddammit!'

Her soft dark eyes focused with extraordinary concentration on his face, and Jack saw her bewitchingly pretty top lip quiver a little before she finally spoke. 'No, Jack... I don't love him. There's only one man I've always loved, and I think you know who that is.'

Her words blew like a warm, gentle wind through his embittered soul and made his heart expand with a joyful lightness the like of which he'd never experienced before. Jack let go of the breath that had tightened so painfully inside his chest and sighed deeply. Tenderly brushing back the ravishing golden hair from her impossibly soft brow, he gazed deeply into the enchanting dark eyes that had haunted his dreams all these years, everything inside him hurting at the sight of the tears that had helplessly misted over them.

'How the hell did I ever live without you?' he grated, just before fastening his hungry, needy mouth to hers.

CHAPTER TWELVE

THERE was such unbounded joy rippling through Caroline's veins at Jack's possessive embrace that she suddenly believed it was possible to fly without wings.

Did he mean the words he had just uttered so passionately? His ravenous kiss told her that he most certainly *did*. The tears that had glazed her eyes trickled softly down her face and into her mouth as Jack's lips melded with hers, his hot silky tongue and dark masculinity tasting like home and heaven at the same time. With his hands expressively showing her how enamoured he was with her curves, it became very clear to Caroline that there was no going back from this point on.

Grinding his hips demandingly into hers, Jack trapped her body against the wall and she willingly surrendered to the seductive opiate of his invading heat. The hotly intense sparks that had been simmering undimmed beneath the hurt and hostility that they had each succumbed to in their turn burst into irresistible flame as their need for each other shattered all bounds of strained politeness. Jack's broad hard chest imprisoned Caroline's breasts as his kiss enraptured her completely, and she worked her hands down between their bodies and mindlessly, hungrily, unfastened the zip of his jeans embedded in soft blue denim. There was no hesitation in the act…no doubt…she simply *had* to… they *had* to…

Pulling her skirt up around her hips as if of the same mind, Jack roughly pushed Caroline's rose-coloured panties down her shivering legs, then inserted himself smoothly inside her, employing a long upwards stroke of voracious male possession.

'You make me—oh, God—you make me *crazy,* Jack…' She moaned into his mouth, stunned by the ferocity of heat that radiated like a blaze inside her.

Her arms wrapped around his neck as his thrusts became more concentrated, then deliberately stopped. He held himself inside her for long, arousing and inflammatory seconds, so that their united pleasure in each other seemed to magnify into an even more achingly deep bliss. Her breath left her body in another deeply affected low-voiced groan.

'Say my name again, Caroline,' Jack taunted against her ravaged lips, his mouth sliding across her face to her earlobe, then down her neck, finally latching in turn onto her tightly budded nipples inside the black velvet top that he so impatiently shoved aside. 'Say my name so that I can hear it's me you want and no one else.'

'Oh, Jack…it's only *ever* been you! There never has been anybody else for me…I swear.'

Jack briefly thought about all the *wrong* turns he'd made personally…the women he'd convinced himself he'd enjoyed—including his ex-wife Anna. None of them had ever produced the uncontained feeling of rapture and untrammelled excitement inside him that Caroline did. Even when he'd been busy blaming her for denying him their child Jack had known underneath it all that he'd never *stopped* loving her…that in fact it was *impossible* for him to do such a thing. He was now convinced that there were some relationships that *absolutely* had to be—no matter how far apart the couple concerned had been, or for how long.

Jack knew for sure that he would love Caroline for ever. How else could he explain the almost instantaneous and soaring heartfelt longing that he'd experienced from the very first moment he'd seen her? It had never just been about lust. Jack *believed* in love at first sight because it had happened to him. Even while he'd so hot-headedly and foolishly denied himself her presence in his life these past seventeen years a secret fever had burned inside him daily—for Caroline.

Now Jack waited until she melted in his arms, and he was the passionate, willing recipient of a heat that was like no other—her soft, rasping sighs turning him on almost to the point of pain, the velvet-textured skin brushing so arousingly up against his own a sensation he never wanted to be free of. Then and *only* then did he allow himself to drive home his own insatiable need for her.

Shaken by the depth of his release, Jack kissed Caroline tenderly on her eyelids, her nose, her mouth, holding her face in his hands and examining her flushed beautiful features with a particularly warm, satisfied smile of undisguised male pride.

'You are *everything* a man could want in a woman and more…you know that?'

'It took you long enough to realise it, Jack.' She raised one finely arched blonde eyebrow, and her soft laughter was infectious.

She was so happy. Her elation flowed through her veins like delightful burgundy wine, flooding all the shadowed places inside her with light and love, and waking up her senses to a world of joy again. Safe in the arms of the man she adored, now there was no doubt in her mind that for both of them their togetherness was for all the *right* reasons.

'I know…but I was a stupid, self-righteous fool who got his comeuppance by consigning myself to endure seventeen long years without you. I didn't only punish you, angel…I punished myself too.'

There was a deeply etched furrow between Jack's dark brows that made Caroline want to kiss every frown he'd ever had away, and bring him so much love and laughter that he'd never need to employ that gesture again.

What was she waiting for? She might as well start

now. Gently, she pressed her lips to the place where that remorseful furrow resided.

'I love you, Jack,' she told him, her heart lifting when an uninhibited smile of pleased satisfaction curved his highly kissable lips.

'I hardly deserve you to… But, however long I live,' Jack began huskily, 'it won't be nearly long enough to show you how much I love *you*, Caroline…and that's a fact.'

'Then we have a great deal of loving ahead of us, wouldn't you say? Let's go up to bed, shall we? I'm anxious not to waste any *more* time.'

Her dark eyes only demonstrating the barest *hint* of shyness, Caroline began to rearrange her clothing and, taking his lead from her, Jack did likewise. Then she took him by the hand and went upstairs with him to her bedroom, just as she intended to do every night for the rest of their lives.

Some time later, in the warm, sated afterglow of their lovemaking, Caroline traced the slender scar on Jack's bare chest tentatively with the tips of her fingers.

Aware of the tension that he suddenly transmitted, Caroline couldn't deny her own underlying unease as she prepared herself to confront him about it. But they had shared the most intimate of intimacies, and if they couldn't share this too then what hope for deepening the trust between them? Glancing up into the handsome face that was both sensitive and troubled now that he had let his guard down, Caroline knew that it was definitely time to get bone-crushingly honest about things.

'Tell me about this, Jack,' she urged, her voice deliberately lowered. 'I need to know.'

She didn't want to exert any pressure, but learning the truth was essential. He sighed, but he didn't push her away or get defensive, as she'd secretly feared he might.

'Six months ago I had a heart attack,' he began, and Caroline hardly dared breathe as she listened intently. 'I'd be a fool if I didn't see it as some kind of serious catalyst for change.'

Absently Jack slid his hand down the side of Caroline's slender bare arm.

'It was entirely self-created. I pushed myself way too hard for far too long. I got rich…but truthfully I derived very little pleasure from the money I made. I discovered to my great shock that there isn't enough wealth and public acclaim in the world to wipe the slate clean of a bitter past. That part was down to *me*. I was still that angry, self-righteous youth who baulked at the cards fate had dealt him…who *despised* being poor. I wanted to show the world that I could rise above anything it cared to throw at me, and in some respects you could say I did. I certainly achieved what I set out to achieve financially…but there was still a gaping hole inside of me the size of the Grand Canyon. Now I know that I should have stayed with you after what happened, instead of using it as a bitter excuse to flee the country. I could have made my fortune anywhere, but I suppose I wanted to get as far away as possible from my past as I could. I'm so sorry, my angel.'

Urging her towards him so that she lay across his chest, Jack kissed her gently on the mouth, his blue eyes blazing at her with profound remorse and love.

Swallowing down the lump inside her throat, Caroline caught his hand and kissed it. 'I know you didn't really mean to hurt me, Jack. I told you—I have no more resentment whatever...*none*. Why don't we just let what happened in the past *stay* in the past, hmm? Today is a new day...a *new* future. Now, tell me about your heart. I want to know the truth, Jack. Are you in any danger still? How can I help?'

Staring up into her concerned brown eyes, Jack felt a wave of warmth permeate his entire being. He had to acknowledge it after all this time—*God had been good to him.* He was still alive, still curious about life, and now he was blessed with the love of the woman he'd thought he had lost for good and had miraculously been reunited with.

'The doctors told me that if I ease my workload and take better care of myself, then I have a damn good chance of living to be old. I'm pretty fit, and still young. Who knows how long I might live if I have the love of a good woman too?' He grinned, and was about to bestow a long, loving, much more leisurely kiss on Caroline's too delectable lips when she deliberately held back and considered him intently.

'Why *did* you come back here, Jack?' she asked

thoughtfully. 'What made you buy your mother's old house and decide to do it up?'

The grin banished, Jack's expression became perfectly serious. 'About a year ago I contacted an estate agency in town to express my interest in the house, should it ever come up for sale. I suppose I had some crazy half-baked notion that one day I might come back and fix it up…just for my own satisfaction. It *haunted* me, losing that house…it *definitely* haunted my mother. I just somehow needed to heal my hurt at it being repossessed all those years ago. Anyway, at the time of enquiring the guy who owned it had no intention of selling. But about a month before I had the heart attack the estate agents rang me to tell me that he had put it on the market. He was moving abroad to Spain and was looking for a quick sale. I bought it there and then. After I got sick, I saw my buying it as some kind of sign that I was meant to go home. I can't explain it…it was just a feeling that came over me. I thought you were long gone…married to some frightfully posh ambitious young doctor in the home counties. But secretly I hoped beyond hope that you might still live here. If you hadn't I would have eventually found you anyway. I'm certain of that.'

Jack let his gaze hungrily roam over her at will, his blue eyes darkening to almost the colour of a perfectly clear night sky. 'Now that I'm here I can see that I was *always* coming back to you, Caroline.'

He was speaking the truth. Ever since he'd suffered the heart attack, Jack had been made frighteningly aware of his own mortality, and pure instinct had sent him back to the woman he loved. The woman he now intended to stay with until he breathed his last breath.

'And what about your ex-wife?'

Jack's hand possessively circled Caroline's wrist as for a fleeting moment he saw doubt reflected in her steady gaze.

'A desperate mistake.' He jerked her a little towards him, so that the soft feathery tips of her ravishing long blonde hair brushed his face. 'I wasn't in love with her, Caroline…I promise you that. Do you believe me?'

She had no reason not to. Even Caroline knew a man in love when she saw one, and Jack truly *did* adore her—she could see that. The tension inside her finally dispersed as she relaxed against his chest.

'I don't blame you for needing the comfort of someone else, Jack. Seventeen years is a long time to be alone…I can personally vouch for that.'

There was no blame in her voice, only a little lingering sorrow that they had waited so long to find each other again.

'You'll never be alone again, sweetheart…not so long as I live and breathe. And even after I'm gone I'll come back and be your guardian angel. So you see? You'll *never* be rid of me.'

Before Caroline could think another melancholy thought, Jack had captured her lips lovingly beneath his own and moved his hands down her body to bring her closer still…

* * *

'You're miles away, Jack…come back to me.'

Smiling up at his serious, preoccupied expression as they walked along the shoreline together, holding hands, Caroline intuitively tried to glean what her husband was thinking about. They had been married for exactly one week and one day, and had wasted no more time in getting to know each other all over again. They had even started finishing each other's sentences, and sometimes accurately guessing each other's thoughts like a long-time married couple.

With every day that passed, Caroline was more and more convinced that destiny had indeed decreed that they were meant to be together. But now, as he stopped on the wet yellow sand and turned to study her, the wind whipping a lock of his thick dark hair across the handsome brow that seemed a lot less troubled and careworn these days Caroline couldn't deny the sudden jolt of anxiety that ran through her blood.

'Jack?'

'I've been meaning to ask…'

'Yes?' For a moment she didn't breathe.

'Did you—did you suffer any *damage* when you had the abortion?' he asked finally.

Feeling shock roll through her, then ebb slowly away, Caroline sighed.

'No…thankfully I didn't. Why are you asking me this now, Jack?'

'I just needed to know. Perhaps it's too early to bring

the subject up… I don't know how you feel about it, but I was thinking…'

'You were thinking that we might try again…for a baby?'

As soon as the words were out, and she saw the look of complete astonishment on his face, Caroline knew she had guessed right. She was so overwhelmed with elation that she could barely speak.

They had been absolutely honest with each other about so many things since they had got together again six weeks ago, and even more so since their marriage, but this was one topic that they had both somehow *avoided*. Caroline knew the reasons why. Past pain had made the subject brittle as glass, and they were still treading carefully around it to avoid being cut. But now they had a God-given opportunity to address it.

'Is it at all possible, do you think?'

Watching her seemingly tussle with the question, Jack tried not to get his hopes up. Now that he was married to Caroline, he couldn't deny his growing desire to be a father, for her to have his baby. But he also knew that she had suffered deep trauma over having been made to have the abortion, and that that trauma had been made worse when Jack had gone away. He could hardly blame her if the idea of becoming pregnant again engendered strong feelings of trepidation and even *fear* inside her.

'I think it's *more* than possible, given the fact that we've been rather lax with birth control,' Caroline replied grinning.

Relieved that she didn't seem too upset about the idea, Jack let his tense shoulders relax.

'So you *like* the idea?'

His arms encircled her waist in her long red wool coat as her bewitching smile grew even wider. 'I *want* us to have a baby, Jack. And this time nobody's going to stop us! In fact…I have a sneaking suspicion that I could be pregnant already. My period's late. I was going to tell you.'

'My God…' His gaze an intensely hopeful gleam, Jack felt something quicken inside him.

'Well, Jack…you've been keeping me pretty busy for the past few weeks. It was *bound* to happen sooner or later, don't you think?'

Examining her shining brown eyes, and seeing the joy that was all but pouring out of them, Jack was suddenly *more* than certain that his wife was carrying their baby inside her.

For a long moment he couldn't speak, he was so moved by the idea that they were to become parents. Then he scooped her up into his arms and swung her round and round right there on the sand, for the world to witness his exultation. It didn't matter that right then there was only an elderly man walking by with his dog. The man smiled at them both indulgently, lifted his cap and walked on, whistling for his dog to follow.

'We'll need a new place to live,' Jack declared when Caroline had laughingly begged him to stop swinging her round because she was getting dizzy.

They had talked about where they would live, of course, but had arrived at no firm decision as yet. Right now Jack was staying at Caroline's place, and work was still in progress on his house. *But they'd agreed they would reside in neither of those places.* They would start afresh somewhere else…somewhere they would both be free from the wounds of the past.

Tomorrow—when the temporary staff that Caroline had hired to look after her shop started work—they were flying out to the Caribbean for their honeymoon. And after that they would fly on to New York, where Jack wanted to introduce his new wife to his friends. He knew already that they would be absolutely captivated by her.

'Could you bear to live by the sea again?' Caroline asked him, her teeth worrying at her soft lower lip.

'I know how much you love the ocean.' Stroking his knuckles gently down the side of her cold windblown cheek, Jack smiled. 'I have a house in California. It's right by the sea. It's rather beautiful, in fact. You would probably fall in love with it, come to think of it. We could always live there.'

Suddenly it didn't matter to Caroline if they lived by the sea or not. As long as she could visit the ocean from time to time, she would be well content.

That settled, she momentarily rested her head against her husband's chest. 'I'm easy,' she said, and smiled.

'Hey,' Jack said jokingly, 'that's not something you should say in front of your husband, *Mrs* Fitzgerald.'

'I love you, Jack.'

'I love you *more*, Caroline.'

'You can't possibly.'

'I'm sorry, but I beg to differ. The love I feel for you can't be measured.'

'Is it deeper than the ocean?' Her lips dimpled teasingly.

'Fathoms deeper.'

'Brighter than the brightest star?'

'More dazzling than Venus herself.'

'That's a whole lot of love, Jack.'

'Isn't that the name of a song?'

He laughed and kissed the top of her head.

'I'll love you for ever, Caroline…that's a promise.'

And, gazing up into her husband's enraptured and loving face, Caroline saw that his impassioned vow was written on his very *soul*…

FREE

4 BOOKS AND A SURPRISE GIFT!

We would like to take this opportunity to thank you for reading this Mills & Boon® book by offering you the chance to take FOUR more specially selected titles from the Modern Romance™ series absolutely FREE! We're also making this offer to introduce you to the benefits of the Mills & Boon® Reader Service™—

> ★ **FREE home delivery**
> ★ **FREE gifts and competitions**
> ★ **FREE monthly Newsletter**
> ★ **Books available before they're in the shops**
> ★ **Exclusive Reader Service offers**

Accepting these FREE books and gift places you under no obligation to buy; you may cancel at any time, even after receiving your free shipment. Simply complete your details below and return the entire page to the address below. You don't even need a stamp!

YES! Please send me 4 free Modern Romance books and a surprise gift. I understand that unless you hear from me, I will receive 6 superb new titles every month for just £2.80 each, postage and packing free. I am under no obligation to purchase any books and may cancel my subscription at any time. The free books and gift will be mine to keep in any case.

P6ZEE

Ms/Mrs/Miss/Mr...Initials ....

BLOCK CAPITALS PLEASE

Surname ....

Address ....

....

....Postcode ....

Send this whole page to:

The Reader Service, FREEPOST CN81, Croydon, CR9 3WZ